CONVERSATIONS
WITH BEETHOVEN

SANFORD FRIEDMAN (1928–2010) was born in New
York City. After graduating from the Horace Mann School
and the Carnegie Institute of Technology, he was stationed as
a military police officer in Korea, earning a Bronze Star. He
began his career as a playwright and theater producer, and
was later a writing instructor at Juilliard and SAGE (Services
and Advocacy for GLBT Elders). "Ocean," a chapter from
Friedman's first novel, *Totempole*, was serialized in *Partisan
Review* in 1964 and won second prize in the 1965 O. Henry
Awards. *Totempole* (1965; available as an NYRB Classic) was
followed by the novels *A Haunted Woman* (1968), *Still Life*
(1975), and *Rip Van Winkle* (1980). At the time of his death,
Friedman left behind the unpublished manuscript for
Conversations with Beethoven.

RICHARD HOWARD is the author of seventeen volumes
of poetry and has published more than one hundred fifty
translations from the French, including, for NYRB, Marc
Fumaroli's *When the World Spoke French*, Balzac's *Unknown
Masterpiece*, and Maupassant's *Alien Hearts*. He has received
a National Book Award for his translation of *Les Fleurs du
Mal* and a Pulitzer Prize for *Untitled Subjects*, a collection of
poetry. His most recent book of poems, inspired by his own
schooling in Ohio, is *A Progressive Education* (2014).

CONVERSATIONS WITH BEETHOVEN

A Novel

SANFORD FRIEDMAN

Introduction by
RICHARD HOWARD

NEW YORK REVIEW BOOKS

New York

THIS IS A NEW YORK REVIEW BOOK
PUBLISHED BY THE NEW YORK REVIEW OF BOOKS
435 Hudson Street, New York, NY 10014
www.nyrb.com

Library of Congress Cataloging-in-Publication Data
Friedman, Sanford, 1928–2010.
Conversations with Beethoven / by Sanford Friedman ; introduction by
Richard Howard.
    pages cm. — (New York Review Books classics)
ISBN 978-1-59017-762-4 (alk. paper)
 1. Beethoven, Ludwig van, 1770–1827—Fiction. 2. Composers—Germany—
Fiction. I. Title.
PS3556.R564C66 2014
813'.54—dc23

                       2014013610

ISBN 978-1-59017-762-4
Available as an electronic book; ISBN 978-1-59017-788-4

Printed in the United States of America on acid-free paper.
10 9 8 7 6 5 4 3 2 1

INTRODUCTION
From the Sidelines

BETWEEN graduating from Horace Mann and earning a BFA from Carnegie Tech, Sanford Friedman wrote seven full-length plays, the first of which was produced when he was nineteen at the University Playhouse on Cape Cod. The subsequent six were never produced nor even published, though I recall reading an arresting melodrama about John Brown which Friedman had written in his early twenties and set great store by to the end of his life.

After his discharge in 1953 from the army—he served as a military policeman in Korea and was awarded a Bronze Star—Friedman and two rather spooky associates leased and renovated Carnegie Hall Playhouse and for two seasons produced plays by, among others, Samuel Beckett, Eugène Ionesco, and Brendan Behan. Revealed as a possibly profitable enterprise, the Playhouse was whisked away from these young, helplessly highbrow producers and, after a questionable stint as Carnegie Hall Cinema, eventually assumed its present, much glamorized guise of Zankel Hall, one of whose occasional highbrow vestiges was to be the Susan Sontag memorial concert.

It was not, however, until 1965 that Friedman published his first novel, *Totempole*, which was a considerable success, even though—or perhaps because—it was the first American fiction whose central character was a sensitive M.P., both Jewish and homosexual. *Totempole* was followed in 1968 by *A Haunted Woman*, the romance of a withering but resourceful actress remarkably "like" Mrs. Jackson Pollock. Then, in 1975, Friedman produced a curiously disparate pair of what his (new) publisher rather cautiously called "short novels": the cover says *Still Life*, but inside we must contend with *Life Blood* as well as *Still Life*—how short can that be? And then, in 1980, yet another publisher presented another (singular) Friedman novel, *Rip Van Winkle*, which turns out to be the recuperation of an American legend which makes that aspiring designation mean what it actually prescribes: this *legend* had better be *read*.

Thereupon follows an extended silence of thirty years until Sanford Friedman voicelessly dies (of a heart attack inside his own front door) in the spring of 2010—but no, I am surely referring to the deliberately stridulent mutism that followed the completion, late in the '80s, of this writer's last (and breathlessly original) novel, remote from any earlier mannerisms and in fact suggestive of the alien designs of Thomas Mann or even W. G. Sebald. The frustrated efforts, over the next twenty years, of this now middle-aged New Yorker to find a publisher for his most ambitious and perhaps finest work were accompanied by a growing rage against the disappointing silence—timidity? repugnance? indifference?—to which it appeared to be condemned.

But this too is a deception: if *The Author proposes his withdrawal, Literature (eventually) presents his triumph.* I believe, deep down, that Sanford Friedman would have been pleased, or at least satisfied, that what he thought of not as his last but rather latest book would, finally, be out in the world with its predecessors. I lived *with* Sanford Friedman for most of the time (nineteen years) during which his books were written; I lived *against* him in the years after. I had many opportunities to observe this remarkable writer and few enough to comfort him, but at least I can point out the wonderful inventiveness of the text of *Conversations with Beethoven*, starting with the title. As most of us know, Beethoven, in the last part of his life, had gone deaf, and the only way anyone could converse with the elderly genius was by scribbling a message, however intimate or formal, in a notebook. Many of such notebooks still survive, and of course the remarkable thing about the "conversations" thus preserved is that the "talk" of everyone *except* the frequently volatile composer is recorded. Beethoven would read the texts and respond aloud (except when he wished to keep his own responses private; at these times the composer himself would write them in another notebook to be shared with only the intended receiver). For the most part, however, the deaf man seems to have been so urgently committed to what he wanted to say, what he wanted done (or not done), that having nothing to go by but the texts of "others," we must imagine, sometimes rather sketchily, what the great man's responses may have been. Though of course Beethoven himself could and did write formal (or informal) letters to be mailed or manually delivered by his own servants...

The wonder of *Conversations with Beethoven*, then, is that each of us must determine its import according to our reading of the words, as Friedman has imagined them, of those who within its pages dare to address the aging, irritable, and eventually hospitalized Maestro—especially his five querulous doctors, his surviving brothers, and his beloved nephew Karl (who has, to his uncle's horror and outrage, ventured to become an officer in the Austrian Royal Army), as well as the boy's hated mother (she closes the "conversations" with an eight-page letter to her son describing Uncle Ludwig's funeral), and a troop of terrorized admirers and musicians (including Franz Schubert) who are more often than not misrecognized by the dying composer, not to mention any number of greedy noblemen eager to be distinguished by the Maestro's dedication of whatever scrap of his immortal music remains unspoken for.

The confounding but entirely convincing procession of these voices can evidently be accounted for by Friedman's early dramatic commitment: perhaps only someone who has written "seven full-length plays" when hardly out of adolescence could have made the voices of his final literary creation so identifiable, so *musical* without footnotes. Perhaps the only explanatory gloss that the reader of *Conversations with Beethoven* should be aware of is the entirely contradictory (and therefore dreadful) amalgam of compassion and contempt for humanity that inspired it. This double entendre might be unrecognizable unless one saw and suffered from it in early and intimate circumstances, as I had occasion to during the many years I lived with the ultimately astonishing novelist Sanford Friedman.

—RICHARD HOWARD
March 17, 2014

CONVERSATIONS
WITH BEETHOVEN

To Tom Lowenstein

It is known that conversation with Beethoven had in part to be written; he spoke, but those with whom he spoke had to write down their questions and answers. For this purpose thick booklets of normal quarto writing paper and pencils were always close at hand.

—FERDINAND HILLER, composer

SPEAKERS	FORM OF ADDRESS
Karl van Beethoven, Beethoven's nephew	Uncle
Karl Holz, a young friend and musician	Maestro
Johanna van Beethoven, Karl's mother	Ludwig
Dogl, a local doctor	Maestro Beethoven
Stephan von Breuning, Beethoven's lifelong friend	Ludwig
Gerhard von Breuning, Stephan's young son	Prospero
Niemetz, Karl's best friend	Mr. Beethoven
Anton Schindler, Beethoven's first biographer	Great Maestro
Johann Wolfmayer, businessman and patron of Beethoven	Dear Friend
Ignaz Schuppanzigh, leader of the Schuppanzigh Quartet	Honored Guest
Seng, an assistant doctor at General Hospital	Mister
Johann van Beethoven, Beethoven's brother	Brother
S. H. Spiker, the Royal Librarian at Berlin	Maestro Beethoven
Michael Krenn, a young servant at Gneixendorf	Master Brother
Therese van Beethoven, Johann's wife	Brother-in-Law
Andreas Wawruch, Beethoven's attending physician	Esteemed Patient
Jakob Staudenheim, a prominent doctor	Celebrated Patient
Johann Baptist Bach, Beethoven's lawyer	Worthy Friend
Giovanni Malfatti, a Viennese doctor	Beethoven
Franz Schubert, a rising young composer	Revered Maestro
Heribert Rau, a banker	Venerated Composer

I

UNCLE,

I keep thinking of the first time I came here. It was the summer after my father died, when you became my father, I mean my guardian, and sent me to Mr. Giannatasio's boarding school. Thus I must have been ten years old—half my years! You took great pleasure in serving as our cicerone, showing us the thermal springs and other sights. I had never seen adults wheeled about in chairs, naturally. How I envied them that luxury (doubtless you will find in this the seeds of my prodigality), until someone told me that those in chairs were either sick or dying. The idea of a watering-place to which adults retired to die was difficult to grasp. Secretly it disgusted me. In any case it was with Mr. G. and his family that I visited you that summer, but later than this, in late August or early September, after my hernia operation. I remember because it was owing to the operation that you forbade me to climb up to Castle Rauhenstein. Somehow or other you had neglected to mention the castle until it loomed overhead. Imagine! a medieval fortress on a hilltop; if Castle Rauhenstein had been the Colossus of Rhodes, I could not have been more excited! I started running up the path, but you stopped me. I begged you to let me go on, but you refused. Tears followed; whereupon you struck me soundly, explaining to the others that during my father's lifetime I would obey only when beaten. If you permitted me to climb up to the castle, I would surely rupture myself once more; it was, you said, for my own good. (How often thereafter did I hear those words! Was it for my own good when, two years later, you pulled me out of a chair so violently that Dr. Smetana had to be sent for?—I had indeed ruptured myself once more!) To temper my disappointment one of the others said that it really made no difference since the castle was nothing but ruins. Needless to say, ten years ago I didn't know the meaning of "ruins."

From the window of this room I can see those ruins in the moonlight; after all these years they beckon still. As a boy, whenever I climbed up there to the tower, I always tried to imagine the dungeon in olden times, before it was buried under silt. Since, however, I had never seen a dungeon, my notions came entirely from illustrations of your *Fidelio*, the Act II mise-en-scène depicting Leonora's rescue of Florestan. In my head I hear the music now, the words are on my lips—Leonora's "Ah, you are saved, thank God!" It never fails to stir me, nor to bring tears. (I should confess that I have had considerable wine; however, lest you reproach me for being profligate, rest assured that it's nothing but a *local table wine*.) "Ah, I am saved, thank God!" sings Florestan. The trumpet, the torches, their glorious duet! Never has there been such sublime music for the stage, unless it is the final chorus in praise of the man who finds a "true wife."

That same year, my first at Mr. G.'s boarding school, an odd-looking man dressed like a ragamuffin showed up one day at the playground. It turned out to be my mother! You and the High Court had forbidden her to visit me; thus she, like Leonora, appeared in disguise. Yet, unlike Leonora, her object was not to rescue me—that would come later; on that occasion she wanted only to set eyes on me and give me her assurances that she had not abandoned me. —Well and good, but did you praise her for her trouble, did you call her a true wife or mother? Hardly! You called her the Queen of the Night; you called her pestilential and a whore!—Not until much later, when I was fourteen and my mother became pregnant with Ludovica, did I even understand the meaning of such slurs. What is more, I had no idea why she christened the baby Ludovica. Later still, when I was old enough to understand, Uncle Johann told me that Ludovica's father was the Hungarian medical student who lodged with us while my own father was still living. Well, needless to say, your brother was misinformed. Only after it became common knowledge that a well-known Finance Councilor had fathered the child, did I finally get up the nerve to ask my mother why she had named Ludovica for you. "To honor him," was all that she said.— Forgive me, I mean no disrespect, yet I cannot help but laugh. *Ludovica!* Was it merely a piece of mischief or was it a clever device to encourage the gossip which was already circulating at the time, namely, that you were in love with my mother? Or, worse still, by naming it Ludovica did she mean to imply falsely that you yourself were the child's father?—Whatever her object, it was not your destiny to find in her or, to be sure, in any other woman, a true wife. Frankly, there were times when I felt convinced that you had settled for *me* in lieu of such a wife, made me your helpmate, housekeeper, amanuensis, as well as the supervisor of the servants, errands, marketing, and God knows what. You even turned me into your wine taster, a kind of variation on the theme of Ganymede, so fearful were you of being poisoned. But you are not Zeus; and I, alas, am still too young to have found a wife. Indeed now I never shall. For God's sake! come to your senses—I am the one imprisoned in that dungeon! *I am Florestan.*

Not since the Congress of Vienna has a Police Chief had a network of *spies* like yours. There is no other term for them, your Holz and Breuning and Schindler, Uncle Johann and Dr. Bach; you even found a way of pressing into service the Director of my school, not to mention my landlord and his wife. Imagine my being forbidden to leave the house after dark without written permission from you—I am twenty years old! Only Talleyrand was ever kept under such strict surveillance. You have even outdone the Secret Police. Instead of your spies informing you of their suspicions, *you inform them;* whereupon they set about to furnish the proof—I suspect the boy is cutting classes, I suspect he is lying and stealing, I suspect him of drinking, gambling, whoring—whatever fancy comes to your mind, and off they rush to catch me in flagrante delicto! Schindler claims to have seen me at the billiard table in a tavern where, he reports, I was not only gambling with some coachmen but cheating them to boot. (How would the sycophant, whom you call Mr. Shitting behind his back, know that I was cheating unless he knows a good deal more about gambling than I do!) Holz bumps into me "quite by accident" at the billiard tables, and voilà! that is all the proof you need. I am called a good-for-nothing, a liar, a swindler, a thief! Such accusations are distressing enough when spoken; they are insupportable when shouted at the top of one's lungs in a towering rage, as is your habit.

Obviously this dungeon in which I find myself is not the place of solitude and silence you have pictured in *Fidelio*; that, alas, is your own dungeon, the dungeon of your deafness. Mine is a place of tumult, of constant violence and shouting. You do not know, nay, cannot know, naturally, the sound of your own voice; sometimes it is louder than fortissimo, louder than the loudest thunderclap! as if in revenge for your deafness you were determined to deafen me.— Apart from the dynamics, you have no idea of your countenance during such outbursts: the ferocity in your eyes, the swelling of your veins, the baring of your teeth—Indeed it is a terrible sight to behold! Yet that is only the half of it. Your rage sets off a kind of blood lust in you, albeit not for blood but tears, my tears; thus you take pleasure in toying with me cruelly, interrogating me like a Grand Inquisitor, tormenting me, torturing me, breaking me down bit by bit, until you take your satisfaction in bringing me to tears!

All of which calls to mind the receipt for this month's room and board. I can only repeat for the hundredth time that I do not have it because *I gave it to you*. Moreover let me state once for all and unequivocally that *I did not embezzle that money*! (Embezzlement, as you used to remind me regularly, is the crime of which my father accused my mother fifteen years ago and for which she was placed under house arrest—never mind that the money "stolen" was her own!) My room and board are paid in full through July. Thus the sum that you are out of pocket is 11 gulden, 10 kreuzer, for Thursday, Friday, today and tomorrow. (Under the circumstances, perhaps the landlord will be good enough to grant you a refund; he is, after all, an honorable man.) Nor have I ever stolen a penny from you! Ha! I can hear you scoff: how about those books of mine that you pawned last month! For that I am deeply sorry; it stains my honor—*for the first and only time*, believe me. I had every intention of redeeming them at the earliest opportunity. Perhaps if you had not been so severe with me in money matters, I would not have been obliged to take them in the first place; nor would I have been driven to wager on my skill at billiards. Regardless of what you imagine, it's simply impossible nowadays for a youth my age to live in Vienna without pocket money. But God in heaven, don't blame my friend Niemetz for corrupting me! By no means is he the "uncouth fellow" that you take him for; on the contrary he is a young man of upstanding character—By the way, did you look in your portable secretaire for the landlord's receipt?—Well, it makes no difference now; after this, you will no longer have to relinquish the bank shares that you bought for me and held on to so tenaciously all these years. Just think! now you can do with them as you please. And may that lay to rest, together with me, your everlasting money worries!

There! the first birdcall. Except for Venus, there is scarcely a star to be seen. Now it is Sunday. In order not to disgrace you, I have put on my best coat and trousers, the ones cut from the English flannel that you bought for me last year. I wish to be buried next to my father, if indeed suicides are permitted burial there. Although I first threatened to take my life in May, I did not in fact buy the pistols until three weeks ago. (I am speaking now of the pair that the landlord found in my room on Friday, not of the ones in the open case before me on the table.) Despite my despondency in May, there was in everything I did and said an echo of Werther, a yearning for what Werther calls "the ecstasy of death." Well, now all that has changed. Now there is no ecstasy, no wish to posture or publish my sentiments—Since yesterday I have been in the power of a mysterious Force. It is that Force which commanded me to pawn the watch you gave me in order to buy these pistols, that Force which made me change into these clothes before boarding the six o'clock coach to Baden. (On my way here I asked myself, wherefore Baden? but to no avail.) It was that selfsame Force which brought me to this room last night, that Force which told me to sit down and write these letters while it was still dark, not to climb up to the castle before daylight.

Now there is a trace of light on the horizon, blue with a tint of rose—it is going to be a lovely day, my last on earth.—Much as I asked myself, wherefore Baden, I now ask wherefore Castle Rauhenstein, why climb all the way up there to put a bullet in my head? Does this, too, relate to *Fidelio*—the unlocking of the cells, the releasing of the prisoners, their brief stroll in the open air? "Only here, here is life," they sing, "prison is a tomb."—Well and good—Yet for me they are indistinguishable—both the open air and the dungeon constitute my tomb.

Basta! says the Force—I would almost wager—*Finish up now*!— Uncannily, its tone of voice—*Finish up*!—But of course! its voice resembles *yours*—Why didn't I—I should have recognized—realized from the start—Yes, yes, it's you, Uncle Ludwig—You are the one who brought me here, who is waiting now—*Finish up*!—waiting so impatiently to lead me up the mountainside, as Abraham led Isaac—Of course!! Now at last I understand—Castle Rauhenstein will be the sacrificial altar at Moriah, and I, your son, the offering— *To what God*, may I ask? In the name of what God are you doing this to me? What angel will intercede on my behalf? What ram— *Basta*!—So be it—Now I am finished—*finished*—

May God forgive you, Uncle.

Your

KARL

2

MAESTRO, I understand your agitation, yet it does no good to vent your wrath on *me*. I am neither your nephew nor his crude companion Niemetz but your devoted friend Holz. Apart from an ardent desire to marry my fiancée next month and to hold my job at the Chancellery, my only object at present is to help you find your nephew.

I am not disputing that. However, just because Karl told his landlord on Thursday that he planned to shoot himself by Sunday, doesn't make it a fait accompli. Sunday has scarcely begun! Besides, not only were the pistols confiscated by the landlord, but Karl told me on Friday he had every intention of returning to his room.

Since we have no other clues, it behooves us to go there at once and question the landlord.

Regardless of whether the man is a churchgoer, early Mass will be over by the time we reach his house.

We are wasting time—let us be off.

———

Revered Composer, unfortunately your nephew did not sleep in his room last night; indeed I have not seen him since Friday morning.

For your sake and, I may say, his I'm terribly sorry that this distressing business continues.—As for the receipt for July's room and board, I have written out a copy for you and marked it paid in full.

Would that I had somewhere else to suggest. Unless—perhaps he is with that disreputable friend of his—Yes, without question I would look for him there, I mean at Mrs. Niemetz's.

May God be with you.

———

Maestro, Mrs. Niemetz asserts he is not in the house.

She insists she hasn't seen him since Thursday when he spent the night.

Please calm yourself!

Depravity aside, the woman is old enough to be Karl's mother.

I didn't know that he had stayed overnight once before. Still, only a Secret Agent would enter by force.

I did indeed ask to speak to the son; she said he was sleeping.

She refused to wake him.

I have no reason to doubt her word; after all, she didn't say he was attending church.

Sometimes women of her type are more truthful than women of virtue.

Your sister-in-law excepted, naturally. In her case—Heavens! we haven't looked for Karl at the most likely place of all, his mother's house. Let us go there at once!

If you won't cross her threshold, you could wait in the bakery across the street.

Then by all means come with me to the door.

In any case it needn't be decided now.

Come, we are wasting time; you'll make up your mind along the way.

———

God be thanked, Maestro, *Karl is here*

Unfortunately he has already made good on his threat.

He is not dead.

In the bedroom with his mother. She urges you to come into the house.

Presumably she has no objection to your seeing him, but only a moment.

———

Please, Uncle, it's useless to ask *why*. I wrote you a letter last night—Niemetz will soon deliver it.

Please don't kneel beside the bed—it's too pathetic.

To *you*—I hardly did it to you! I am the one with a bullet in his head.

For God's sake, don't torment me with tears and reproaches. It's done! "What's done is done." What's needed now is a surgeon, in particular a man who knows how to hold his tongue.

Mother has already sent for someone.

Naturally, Ludwig, a doctor was sent for at once.

No, not Smetana—I sent for Dr. Dogl.

He is just as respected as S. and lives much nearer.

Shh! let us step out—Karl must rest.

———

Ludwig, do sit down until the doctor comes. You look so pale—would you like a schnapps?

I understand—But even so, it's eleven years since your brother died in this house.

Be still! I will not discuss the matter in front of a stranger—please send Mr. Holz out of the room.

It makes no difference that Holz obliged—I will not discuss the matter under any circumstances.

Come to your senses—*my son is dying*

Not again! Instead of fabricating my part in your brother's death, you would do better to ponder yours in your nephew's suicide.

Spare me that shit—I won't hear another word!

———

Maestro, not only does she refuse to rejoin you, but she demands that you leave the house.

If you won't apologize, at least refrain from speaking of your brother's death.

Do lower your voice or she'll hear you.

I'm not taking her part. Yet after what has happened, it's essential for you to cooperate with her; otherwise *you* will be the one to suffer.

Well and good, I'll try to smooth things over.

———

Ludwig, before we go on I'll thank you to remember that your brother died of consumption, *not at my hands*! Hardly had he breathed his last when you demanded that an autopsy be performed. The doctor, lest you forget, was a personal friend of yours. Even so, he found no grounds for your abominable suspicion that I had poisoned your brother—I will not put up with these repeated accusations.

In that case let us go on. A teamster, God be thanked! found the boy and carried him down from the ruins at Baden.

Less than half an hour ago. I sent the man on to your place with a note explaining what had happened—obviously you didn't receive it.

The name is *Dogl*—I have no idea what could be keeping him.

By all means send for Dr. Smetana—whichever man arrives first will do the job. But one thing is of the utmost importance—regardless of who it is, *he must not report what happened.*

Because they will surely take Karl away, and if he is moved—Well, I fear the worst!

VIENNA, JULY 30, 1826

Most honored Doctor Smetana,

A terrible misfortune has occurred, a misfortune which *Karl* has accidentally brought upon himself. I hope there is still a chance to save him, but my hope depends particularly on you, provided you can come soon. Karl has a *bullet* in his head. How this happened, you shall learn in due course—But quickly, for God's sake, quickly.

Yours respectfully,
BEETHOVEN

As help had to be provided quickly, he had to be taken to his mother's where he now is. I enclose her address.

Maestro, the man who just arrived is Dr. Dogl. He asks that you remain in here until he finishes.

Yes, but first he must shave the wounded area.

Shall I dispose of the note to Smetana?

In that case I'll deliver it now and return without delay.

Maestro Beethoven, I'm greatly honored to meet you.

So far so good; I have removed the bullet and dressed the wound. Still, I would be deceiving you, were I to say he is out of danger. Far from it! In truth his life is in the balance.

At this moment I have no way of knowing the condition of his brain. If the brain has been injured, the signs may not appear until next week, in which case he is lost.

You misunderstood me, I didn't say he is lost *at present*, nor that the signs are *certain to appear*; we can only wait and see. So far there is no fever; if it comes that will be the turning point.

As for this other matter of not informing the authorities, I'm afraid I can't oblige your sister-in-law; to do so would finish me as a surgeon. Surely you understand.

The best I can do is to delay your nephew's removal from the house.

To the prison ward of the hospital.

Naturally, it goes without saying that suicide is looked upon as a criminal act.

If you'll excuse me, I'll say good-bye now to your nephew.

———

Maestro, I have word from Dr. Smetana. He considers Dr. Dogl altogether capable and will not come to Karl unless Dogl requests a second opinion.

It can't be helped, you know the way of doctors.

Dr. Dogl is leaving now—he says he'll look in again tomorrow.

While you were seeing him out I read what he wrote. In view of that, I suppose it would be best for us to go the police ourselves.

If you wish, but frankly you look spent. Would it not be better for me to go there on my own and report back to you?

D'accord! I'll wait while you say good-bye to him.

Presumably she is with Karl.

For heaven's sake, that is no reason not to say good-bye. By all means go in.

———

Maestro, what is it, what happened inside?

But *something* caused your tears.

Don't continue—she has come into the room.

Ludwig, presumably you understand that my object was not to hurry you but to keep Karl from growing agitated—in his condition that would be the worst thing possible. If indeed I pushed you, I apologize.

It's not for me to explain why your "son" refuses to speak to you—if he lives, perhaps he'll explain the matter himself.

I know nothing of the letter entrusted to Niemetz.

It would be best for you to leave now—Holz is fetching your hat and stick.

Maestro, your sister-in-law is right; do leave now. I will delay a moment and find out what I can of why Karl won't speak to you. Then I shall attend to the matter we discussed earlier.

———

Maestro, you were wise not to come with me to the police; the officiousness and the posturing were extremely tedious. As you already know from Dr. Dogl, suicide is punishable by law.

Karl will receive a serious reprimand and be placed under police surveillance; worse still, you yourself, as guardian, will have to appear before the Magistrate tomorrow.

Of course I shall accompany you.

Although I persuaded her to let me have a word with him, your nephew was anything but helpful.

With regard to his unwillingness to speak to you, he merely said, "if only you would stop reproaching him."

Believe me, that is more or less the sum of it.

There will be time enough tomorrow to discuss the rest.

Please don't insist upon

Well then, he also said, "if only you would never show your face again."

If you do, he threatens to tear off the bandage!

In my view he is suffering some sort of delirium; your sister-in-law mentioned that Dr. Dogl

No, in truth he is not delirious. As you well know, I don't always regard your nephew as deserving of your devotion. If you were not so kindhearted, you would have sent him packing long ago. But never mind, your sister-in-law gave me this for you.

Dear Ludwig,

Before Dr. Dogl left, he told me that Karl would be allowed to stay here for a week at most. Do let us make a bargain. If you agree to let him stay with me and not visit, *not even once* during this critical period, I give you my word that I will abide by *all your future wishes*. Please, for the sake of Karl whom we both love, agree to this.

Yours

JOHANNA

Maestro, since it is only for a week, I urge you to agree.

Good! Now let us have something to eat and call it a day; you have been through a terrible storm.

Never! you will not find yourself "shipwrecked" while I am alive.

———

Prospero, I hope I'm not disturbing you.

My piano lesson is not until 5:30.

I'm still using Pleyel until the translation of Clementi's *System* arrives.

I was in fact just sitting down to practice when Mother asked me to bring you this.

Dear Ludwig,

I cannot tell you how upset I am by what you said about Karl when I bumped into you on the esplanade this morning; I have never seen you in such a state—all at once you seemed a man of seventy. Please come and have dinner with us today at the usual time, 2 o'clock; it will be just Gerhard and the girls and us (to start with we are having one of your favorites, scrambled eggs and brains). During this trying time, Stephan and I would like you to dine with us as often as you wish, indeed take *all* your meals with us. And rest assured that it will be no imposition; after all, you are not only Stephan's oldest friend, but practically a member of the family. Besides, it is but 27 steps from your front door to ours, as Gerhard never tires of telling us. You cannot imagine how happy it would make *him*, your Ariel, to see you every day; the mere idea of this invitation had him hopping about like one of those performing monkeys in the menagerie, so much does he worship you.—Sometimes it is hard for me to believe that he will be 14 next month.

Your devoted
CONSTANCE VON BREUNING

Yes, Prospero, Mother told me what happened.

I lowered my head not because I'm ashamed, but because I'm sorry.

Not for your nephew, for you, naturally.

Please excuse my impudance but I'm certain you are wrong; your nephew surely ~~reveran~~ worships you.

Father says I spell like a guttersnipe.

I'm so pleased! I'll run and tell her that you accept the invitation.

———

Ludwig, clearly you interest Gerhard a good deal more than his lessons do; I had to remind him that dinner was over ten minutes ago.

I am not obliged to return to the War Department for another quarter of an hour; I'll just have Constance send the girls to their room so that we may have some privacy.

In truth I have not seen your nephew all summer, except in passing; thus I have no idea what could have prompted him to do such a thing.

If I remember correctly, he was expected to take his examinations at the end of June.

I did in fact hear some talk of gambling debts.

By no means from him, nor did he approach me for a loan.

Believe me, I am withholding nothing. If I appear reserved, that is because I have learned my lesson. During our lifelong friendship we have fallen out three times, and each time the cause pertained to your nephew or, on one occasion, to his father. Our most recent quarrel, which I need hardly remind you took nine years to patch up, resulted from my opposition to your becoming the boy's guardian. In all likelihood neither of us has enough years left for a repetition of that.

I would have you pay attention to yourself for a change. Only by luck, or rather, a miracle did you finish the new quartet on the Friday before this business occurred. And you have told me there is to be a fifth quartet, to say nothing of the Requiem for your friend Wolfmayer, your Saul & David oratorio etc. Consider how much work you still wish to do. Besides, you are not in the best of health.

"A little abdominal trouble," indeed; inflammation of the bowels is a serious matter. Why, you suffered an attack as recently as January. Everything cannot concern Karl; you must look after yourself as well.

In my opinion you ought to go away. For the first time in twenty-five years you have failed to leave town for the summer, yet both of us know that your welfare depends entirely upon your doing so.

I trust that you are mistaken and that your nephew will soon recover.

I am not recommending that you go to Baden, surely not after what has just happened, nor that you leave tomorrow, but I do believe

Before which Magistrate must you appear?

At what time?

Would you like me to accompany you?

No, not with Holz; there is no need for two of us.

If I made a face, it's because, well, frankly I don't trust your Mr. Holz—nor am I alone in that.

It's time for me to return to my work. When you learn the Magistrate's name, let me know; it may be that I have met the man and could approach him on your behalf.

———

Maestro, Magistrate Czapka says he is an admirer of your music.

Under the circumstances it might be better for you to write your responses and I shall answer for you.

Czapka says he admires the violin sonatas most of all, especially op. 24, which he and his wife play frequently—There you have a promising sign!

I would find it more promising if he had cited op. 47

Most of what he just finished saying you already know. There is but one new stipulation: since Karl's offense is a crime against the church, he will be consigned to the care of a priest for "instruction."

They would do better to instruct his mother!

There will be no instruction while he is at his mother's; it will begin only after the police remove him to the hospital.

No police!!! I will not have it!

Keep in mind that Karl is under arrest.

Tant pis! *I will not suffer the disgrace of their coming to my sister-in-law's in broad daylight for all the world to see—Never! Request that I be allowed to arrange for his removal myself.*

Czapka says that such a request is highly irregular, but he will take it under advisement.

Tell him that if the police dare

Prudence, I beg of you! We may yet be obliged to contest other, more critical issues—Czapka just finished explaining that if Karl survives, the Magistracy will conduct a hearing into the causes of the act.

They have no business to conduct

Czapka says that you are free to go.

I didn't know I had been charged with a crime!

Instead of objecting, this is the moment to thank the Magistrate and show him your most dazzling smile.

Bravo! You have won the man completely. By the way, may I know which bagatelle you plan to bestow upon the wife?

Who knows, I'll fabricate something. Meanwhile my only plan is to go straight home and resume work on the new quartet.

Under the circumstances, will it be possible for you to work?

Under the circumstances, work is the only possibility!

———

Mr. Beethoven, please forgive me for disturbing you, but Karl left me instructions to bring you this letter.

I am unaware of any "secret" motive he may have had, perhaps the letter will disclose one.

I don't understand what you are driving at.

On the contrary, Karl is perfectly *sane*.

I didn't know he suffered from headaches as a child; he hasn't complained of one recently.

I beg your pardon but that is unjust; in no way am I responsible for what has happened.

What evil influence?

I taught him nothing! As you know, Karl and I met at boarding school when we were thirteen years old; what we learned thereafter, we learned *together*.

You may say what you like about Karl's mother, but I'll thank you not to defame *mine*!

Suspicions be damned! Good day.

———

VIENNA, AUGUST I

Karl!

Your filthy carrier pigeon has brought your letter. However reluctant I am to put my answer in writing, I have no choice but to do so since I am forbidden to set eyes on you—Dear God, *why*? Am I plague-ridden!!! Must I rely solely on Holz for news of you? What if you took a turn for the worse—God forbid! and needed—Away with such thoughts! If you don't survive, neither shall I; believe me, that will be my end—And you speak of tears! How dare you accuse me of lusting after—Faugh, the shame of it! Are you not in your right mind? What do you know of tears! Since I became your guardian I have shed more tears than the grieving Niobe. Why, on Sunday alone—Basta!—But that is to speak in the voice of your mysterious *force*—Spare me such madness—Alas, I do believe that you *are* insane—Just imagine! accusing me of forcing you—of being the force—How dare you hold me to blame—I, who would not have harmed—nay, would have done anything, *anything*—who wanted only—I would have only to take care of you   Speaking of tears, voilà! you see where mine have stained the page.

I will now refresh your memory with regard to certain past events—I was at great pains to plan your education, ever bearing in mind the kind of education that I myself did not receive—But make no mistake, it was not through any fault of my father's! On the other hand is not a son's education the foremost responsibility of a *true father*? (Never mind for now the responsibilities of a true mother.) I sent you to the best schools, regardless of the cost or sacrifice to me; I paid for your tutors and piano lessons and always saw to it that you needed for nothing—Why, I even tried to provide for you beyond the grave, a kindness for which you now see fit to ridicule me—No! I do not wish to keep the bank shares—I do not want them! *They are yours!*—To whom would I give them in any case, to my wretched un-brotherly brother? Never! your Uncle Johann is a moneybags already. Those shares were bought for you, held for you, retained even when I was up to my eyes in debt (including a debt of your mother's which I took upon myself) and was threatened with a lawsuit. Pressed on all sides I turned to my brother, naturally, to whom else could I turn? But brother Cain refused to guarantee a loan for me! Thus was I obliged against my will (obliged, note well, by the force of neces-sity, not by a delusory force) to sell a share. Nevertheless I held on to the rest like an eagle, gripping them tightly in my talons—for you! for no one but you did I hold them, as though to honor a sacred trust.

As for your *true mother*—If indeed you are Florestan, then I must be Leonora seeing that I am the one who rescued you from your vi-cious or, rather, your unworthy mother's influence. Besides, the ac-tion was taken, as you well know, in full compliance with the terms of your father's will. Admittedly I called your mother the Queen of Night and taught you to do the same; if, however, I called her a whore, I did so only after you were old enough to understand the term and, I may say, only after the woman had sold herself for 20 gulden on every dance floor in Vienna! What is more, she had given birth to *two* illegitimate children! Why, you yourself—For discre-tion's sake I have always taken care to conceal the fact that you your-self narrowly escaped a similar fate, inasmuch as your mother was three months' pregnant when your father married her! Still, she does not hold a candle to your Aunt Therese who had in tow a bas-tard five years old when my brainless brother married *her*!

Easy virtue aside, I always took care to instill in you but one idea with regard to your mother, namely, that *you should honor her*. In my day that was the only fashion in which children were permitted to behave. Obedience was deemed one's duty, pure and simple. By God, if a man takes it upon himself to house, feed, clothe and educate a child, that man is clearly the child's parental benefactor; therefore he is deserving of unqualified respect and gratitude, to say nothing of submission—Never in my life did I talk back to my father. Nor did I ever contradict him or even voice a demur. I was always docile and ready to do as I was told. If he made me practice until midnight, I did as I was told; if he woke me at two in the morning, routed me out of bed and ordered me to practice until dawn, I did as I was told. Even so, I was beaten all but daily—not only did he beat me but—By the way, the punishment was meted out with your grandfather's walking stick, the very one that I myself carry to this day. Yet worse than the beatings, far worse—he often locked me

I have violent diarrhea today, indeed I have had it since your dis-appearance Friday—Well now, where was I? Yes yes, I was recalling those times when my father locked me up in the cellar—a fiendish place! Not only was it black as pitch, but cold and damp and rat-infested; besides I was only five or six years old, whereas you are nearly twenty—And you have the audacity to speak of dungeons. What do you know of dungeons?! Why, the one you speak of is merely an engraving, and the prisoner merely a performer posturing upon a stage. Moreover you style my deafness a dungeon. Well, in that regard you are partly right. Yet to speak of the silence and the solitude en passant as if—Solitary confinement!!! That is a punish-ment whose harshness you cannot possibly imagine. In the begin-ning I fancied that I was like the rest of you, *in spite of my secret*—Ha! so much for self-delusion! Simply because I was free to take walks, enter drawing rooms or attend the theater, did not signify that I was released from the cellar—I mean cell. Far from it! No matter where I go or what I do, those walls are always with me; they cut me off from everyone, imprison me inside myself—Enough!

I cannot help but suspect that you too, my thankless son, have a *secret*, one so shameful that you dare not share it with anyone, unless with that vulgar, dissolute companion of yours—Well, go on then, share it with N but not with your devoted father—Come to your senses! you must share it with me. Somehow or other I will find it in my heart to understand and forgive you, regardless of the impropriety. And bear in mind that I myself once contemplated suicide, that I too once had a secret—*What is yours?* Confide in me, I implore you! Even if it pertains to women or, worse, to an *older* woman—It so happens that Mrs. N let drop that you spent the night on

———

Great Maestro, please forgive the interruption, I did not mean

———

Please not be angry Mister Beethoven—he make me bring this.

Great Maestro,

I would ask you not to scold the housekeeper for bringing you this. Since, however, you ordered me out of the room I feel obliged to account for my behavior. I truly regret having startled you, but believe me I was *not* trying to spy on you, nor did I read a word of what you were writing. Hence I entreat you to see me again, however briefly, if only to let me reassure you that your former Secretary-sans-salary remains your most loyal and devoted

SCHINDLER

I fetch him

———

Great Maestro, you have my heartfelt thanks for permitting me

Alas, I realize that things will never be the same with us, not at least while Holz is with you. But perhaps after his impending marriage

You misunderstand, my tears are not for myself.

For *you*—I have not seen you so dispirited, nay, *bowed*.

I am indeed aware of what has happened; nevertheless you must have faith that your nephew will recover.

In my view it was the examinations, his failure to

Well and good, but after giving up his studies at the University, for him to have failed his first examinations at the Polytechnic Institute

All the same I am convinced it was the examinations.

Gossip concerning whom?

Most everyone I know is in complete sympathy with you; only one or two hold you to blame.

It makes no difference; they are people of little

Please don't aggravate yourself, it's hardly worth

———

Maestro, was that not Schindler I saw skulking away?

No one of sound mind holds you to blame. The man is a fool!

Rest assured that I will not abandon you after my marriage. Besides, what makes His Bossiness assume that you are ready to take him back?

Yes, I just came from there. Your sister-in-law says that Karl's condition is unchanged.

If it were worse, she would hardly say

But he is *not* worse.

Your sister-in-law aside, do not forget that it's your *nephew* who is holding you at bay.—With regard to our little party this week

I changed the subject only because I have nothing more to say in that connection. Do let me report on the party.

Firstly our overlarge host, the renowned violinist Milord Sir John Falstaff Schuppanzigh, has postponed the event for one night in order to accommodate Vienna's premier cloth merchant, your good friend and patron Wolfmayer.

On the contrary the delay brings a happy outcome: our own lame Oedipus, the salty and celebrated violoncellist Linke will now be able to attend.

Unfortunately Weiss is still indisposed; but even so, on hand will be three members of the Schuppanzigh Quartet, including your humble servant and second fiddle Holz.

No, Dr. Bach was not free.—Now for savory matters, Wolfmayer insists upon bringing the drinks.

Champagne, Moselle and a Hungarian red!

smoked salmon, trout, meat salad and macaroni with Parmesan cheese

As for the dessert, not a word was said.

I have no idea, it's to be a surprise.

Believe me, Milord Sir John would not say; it will come as a surprise to me as well.

––––––––

Maestro, why even a street Arab could answer your query—obviously there is a top hat, a frock coat, a waist

I, Holz, imbibe too much? Come now, how often have I heard you yourself say that *one can never have too much champagne*! Besides, unless I have lost count, I am no more than a glass ahead of my most honored and excellent master.

Yes, yes, the apparel—Apparently the apparel is a gift from your friend apparent Wolfmayer. I urge you to examine the top hat; it appears to be made of spaghetti.

If you doubt me, let us ask the manufacturer himself.

––––––––

Spaghetti indeed, Ludwig; it's lacquered cane loosely woven to release the summer's heat; the frock coat, too—the cloth is something new from our factory in Tulln; it's lighter in weight than worsted—partly wool, partly goat hair.

I trust that you are not just saying so to please me. Some self-styled wit has already dubbed it "lettuce." In my view the color is effectual because it *appears* cool. Besides when worn with the white silk waistcoat—Well, merely to behold it causes chilblains! Please do me the honor of slipping it on.

Maestro, you have stepped from the pages of our fashion journal! Come, allow me to escort you inside to Milord's dressing mirror so that

Will my Honored Guest not have his host, Milord Sir John escort him to my bedchamber?

Indeed I said no such thing—Capacious though my bed is, there is hardly room for me within its confines, let alone himself besides!

What is the meaning of this? While all of us agree that he looks handsome, strikingly handsome in his new top hat and frock coat, my Honored Guest stands before his image in tears! Champagne is meant

Ludwig, what is the matter, why did you send the others from the room?

I'm pleased that you like the apparel. However, this is not the first time that I have done something of the sort, yet tears were not shed formerly.

Holz is right, I did cry like a child over the adagio, the more when I heard the cavatina. But what

Come now, dear friend, there is quite a difference between a frock coat and a string quartet!

Well and good, I don't deny that we both excel at what we do, yet given the choice I would prefer to excel at what you do.

On the contrary it is I who am in *your* debt.

Please remember that when I commissioned you to write the Requiem you were working on your Mass; after that came the choral symphony, and now the quartets

I know little of your other patrons but as for myself, I neither need nor shall I miss 100 ducats. Besides, once the quartets are finished, there will be ample time

Do not say that. After all, you are only 56 years old; many works remain

Be patient please, you'll feel quite differently as soon as your nephew

I have no idea, who but God can say what prompts someone to commit such an act?

I have heard the gossip about his gambling debts and the failure to pass his examinations, yet ever since Werther—Well, I cannot help but suspect that the cause concerns love.

Nothing, rest assured that I have heard no such gossip.

Do believe me, please.

Finished—the C sharp minor quartet?

But no one said a word to me.

I'll keep it to myself, naturally. Was it finished before your nephew—

Goodness, only three days before—Surely the work of Providence!

Better, you say? Forgive me, but I simply cannot imagine a work better than the B flat quartet.

To *me*?

The dedication of your new quartet—I'm hardly deserving

But a work of such importance

My apologies, Ludwig. Now you have seen for yourself the manner in which I cried over your cavatina

Excuse me, someone is calling from the other room.

It was Schuppanzigh, he wished to know which of us was on top.—
Instead of Falstaff, perhaps you should start calling him Doll
Tearsheet.

He also said that dessert is being served.

———

Honored Guest, it is nothing more than an apricot cream.

Alas, I'm not at liberty to reveal the recipe.

It was obtained at a certain Konditorei from a certain waiter who
made me swear an oath never to show it to anyone—unless in my
waistline!

Maestro, if it's still this hot in September, will you lend me your new
top hat for my nuptials?

To relieve the heat of the day

Doubtless the heat of the night will be welcome!

How kind of you, but the member I have is quite sufficient.

Speaking of size, Milord Sir John would have a word with you.

Honored Guest, I too have a request to make.

Will he not lend Milord his frock coat?

Maestro, beware—the seams will not hold.

While I replenish your glass, there is yet another mendicant, namely, Oedipus.

Modish Maestro, am I the only one who covets the waistcoat? It is truly elegant.

Frankly I can't say. Although I'm taken for a gossip, I alone among the guests entertain no theory why your nephew committed the act.

If he continues to maintain his silence, perhaps you should consult Tiresias.

Forgive me, I made light of it only because I understand the gravity. Have you any idea when he'll be removed to the hospital?

But since there are no signs as yet of brain injury, you ought not

Honored Guest, I'm afraid that our little party is an utter failure.

In view of the fact that he was invited chez moi to *take his mind off his nephew*, all that we have spoken of

Maestro, pay no attention to Milord; surely it would be easier to take Jacob's mind off Benjamin.

Then perhaps it's time to say good night—Come, I'll see you home.

I stand corrected or, strictly speaking, I stand unsteadily—indeed it's Beethoven who will see Holz home!

———

VIENNA, AUGUST 4, 1826

Dear Ludwig,

Thank you for honoring our agreement. The Police have now informed me that they will remove Karl to the general hospital early Monday morning. He will be kept in a room on the three-gulden floor; a deposit is required for sheets, towels, utensils etc. Not only will I attend to his personal linens and other personal effects, but I shall do my best to pay my share of the charges.

As you well know, six days have passed without the least sign of improvement; nevertheless Dr. Dogl cautions that it may take yet another week or even two before the boy is out of danger—May God grant the swift arrival of that day!

Yours

JOHANNA

———

Most Excellent Second Violin!

In spite of my request to bring Karl to the hospital myself, the police will not hear of it. Thus I must find a bigwig to help me. However, I cannot for the life of me lay my hands on the name of the Magistrate we saw last Monday—What a pity that Breuning doesn't know the man—And how unfortunate that you, dear Romeo, are slipping off to Baden tomorrow!

In the greatest haste, your

BEETHOVEN

———

Dear Maestro,

The Magistrate's name is Czapka. Although I shall return from Baden Sunday night, I must be at the Chancellery first thing Monday morning. But rest assured that I shall be in touch with you Monday afternoon.

Your most devoted

HOLZ

———

Esteemed Second Violin!

Czapka was unwilling to alter the Magistracy's regulations—So much for the bagatelle I promised the wife! In order to keep out of sight, I went into the bakery to witness Karl's removal. His mother, on the other hand, chose to oversee the whole affair from the street, thereby calling attention not only to herself, but to the family's disgrace. As for the police, they did their duty with dispatch, yet when it came time to transfer Karl to the waiting cart they handled him in the most barbaric fashion! The cart itself was strangely reminiscent of the sapling carts the French used in 1809 to bring their wounded into the city—Suddenly I see myself in my brother's cellar, the place where I took refuge from the howitzers during the seige. Although Karl was only three years old at the time, it was during that infernal night and the next day that I came to know the imp—Again and again he would sneak up on me in the shadows and tug at the pillow which was wrapped around my head—I held it there to protect my ears from the noise of the shells. He didn't understand, naturally. Thus it became a game for him to try and pull the pillow off. At first I was put out by such behavior in a child; so, too, was his father, who gave him quite a smack. Yet after some tears the game resumed, and when the little rascal began calling me his rabbit—well, I lost my heart to him! And now he is carted off like a prisoner! The devil take them all—

Your

BEETHVN

———

Maestro, Dogl was right, Karl is still in danger; however, the injury to the periosteum is only

The bone-covering—the injury is only superficial.

Two nurses watch over him every minute.

Not because of his condition, but rather to forestall another suicide attempt—

Do try to be patient about visiting him.

It's not simply a question of his willingness; he is not always conscious.

Yes, alas, that still remains a possibility.

By law he would have to be buried outside the cemetery, in unconsecrated ground.

At Rabenstein, the place set apart for suicides—

———

Maestro, I regret to say that his recovery is still in doubt.

By no means, his care leaves nothing to be desired; four of the ablest doctors visit him four times a day.

———

Maestro, I bring you wonderful news—*Karl is out of danger*!

It might be better to wait; thus far your patience has been exemplary.

I have reason to believe that tomorrow will be too soon.

In truth he is still unwilling to see you.

He gave no reason.

You are absolutely right. As you know, I would be the last to defend your nephew's behavior.

Wait and see, he'll relent. Meanwhile the Magistrate will now assign a priest to him.

For purposes of instruction.

———

Maestro, the housekeeper told me you were here; she said to look for you at your "most adorable coffee house."

I can only suppose that she meant most adored.

There are just too many ears here; let us write everything.—Firstly, the Magistrates will hold another hearing on August 30th.

No more hearings!!!

It's unimportant, only the topmost pages got wet.

Do stop fussing—the waiter will mop up the rest

To come back to the Magistrates, they consider it their duty to investigate the suicide attempt.

Never! How dare they schedule such a hearing—what gives Czapka the right!

As Chief Magistrate, he has the right

To shit, as the rest of us do—I'm still Karl's guardian and nothing, not even Empty Emperor Franz, gives Czapka the authority to interfere in my affairs. Never again will I permit my linen to be aired in public— Never!!! I had more than my fill of that when the court got rid of the depraved mother and appointed me sole guardian

Apropos of the guardianship, for the sake of your health and your peace of mind I urge you to resign.

For the sake of yours, I urge you to drop the subject

But I am not alone of that opinion, it's shared by Dr. Bach and Councilor Breuning.

Five minutes ago you wrote firstly—let us proceed to secondly

A priest has been assigned to Karl; he is said to be a skilled casuist, as well as very strict.

Of what order?

Redemptorist

As you know, I find their mysticism a trifle brainless—Still, I don't much care if the man is a contortionist, providing he gets to the bottom of Karl's secret.

If anyone can, it's these Redemptorists.

Unless my nephew proves more cunning than the priest

You may be surprised; these men are like leeches, and their methods can be medieval.

Torture???

Rest assured that the line is drawn there.

How long will the "instruction" last?

That depends on your nephew. Even when the doctors are quite ready to send him home, he will not be released until the priest obtains a profession of conversion.

If I know my Karl, the profession will be imminent by the end of next week.

He must also pass a religious examination.

Don't forget how quick-witted the boy can be when it suits him—He'll be out of there in time for his name day!

When is that?

September 4th—Preparations must be made

He cannot possibly be released before—What is the matter? Have you only now spotted Secret Agent Schwenke?

I have made up my mind—I'll visit Karl this week

But he is still not

Let us pay and leave this most adorable nest of spies!

———

Yes, that is correct; the patient is on the three-gulden floor in the surgical section.

When you get there ask for Assistant Dr. Seng.

———

Mister, do speak up, I can bearly hear you.

Yes, I am Dr. Seng.

Now you are shouting—it's forbidden to disturb the patients. Do you know how to write?

From your appearance I wouldn't have guessed that you were literate—Then take the pencil, and please be quick about it—I'm on my rounds.

I'm looking for my nephew, a young reprobate—a good-for-nothing

Does the fellow have a name?

Naturally, but one that he has dishonored—Beethoven

You—surely you are not the great Beethoven?

Surely I am—Is he in your charge?

Yes, Mr. Beethoven

I really had no wish to visit him since he doesn't deserve it. In addition to being utterly spoiled and worthless, he is all but ruined morally. Besides, he has brought me nothing but aggravation. If I were wiser, I wouldn't have come but he begged me to do so.

Let me assure you, Mr. Beethoven, that I have given your nephew the best possible care from the start and will continue to do so while he is here—You have my word on that.

In what room will I find the scoundrel?

Please follow me, I'll take you to him.

Uncle, I told Holz that I would let you know as soon as

You may request one from the Matron, or sit on the edge of the bed, as you wish.

It's not permitted. The door is never closed except when the priest comes in to instruct me; otherwise I am kept under constant surveillance—Thus it would be best for you to write your part.

I have brought with me my answer to your demented letter—However, if the door must remain open, we'll speak of that another time—Well now, is this what I'm paying 3 gulden for, this crypt! Or should I say dungeon, a subject on which you deem yourself an expert! How asinine to place the window all the way up there—one can't even look outside.

At least there is daylight now, it's worse at night.

How so?

It's impossible to sleep because of vermin, not to mention my fellow patients.

What mischief are they up to?

Not only do they guzzle wine and schnapps

But surely that is forbidden

Naturally

Perhaps your priest should also be instructing them.

They are the most common people; I simply cannot imagine how those in the ward behave. Thank you so much for keeping me in a room.

So now I'm to be thanked—Spare me your toadying! I have read your rantings with regard to being in prison, albeit in a delusory one—Well, now you are in a true prison! Moreover, you came to it through an act of your own commission—Why??? What made you do it? I want the truth!

Although I'm out of danger, my condition is still extremely poor. Since nothing can be changed, the less said about what happened, the better.

But you owe me an explanation

I would ask you not to pound the mattress; the result is comparable to your pounding my head.

Then tell me the truth! What are you concealing?

Nothing—On my word I have told you everything.

Rubbish! Your everlasting lies have debased your word.

The Sister asks you to excuse the interruption.

What did she want?

Ostensibly to see how I was faring; yet I suspect that she wanted to have a look at the famous composer.

Thanks to you the famous composer is done for!

Come now, Holz mentioned the gift of a new frock coat from Wolfmayer; why are you dressed in your shabbiest one?

For reasons that you are too callow to understand.

For example?

Shame! I'm ashamed of my worthless nephew! Hence I wished not to call attention to myself—But we are wasting time. In short order you'll be released from this prison—What do you intend to do with your life?

Whatever pleases you; I'm still your ward.

Damnation!!!

What is the matter? I beg you not to make a scene.

Although you no longer regard yourself as my son, you are still my—by blood! you are my nephew and will remain such forever

Let us continue, Uncle.

To reiterate, what career do you plan to pursue?

Since my choice has caused such bitter quarrels in the past, I hesitate to answer.

Coyness has no place in one verging on twenty—Out with it!

A military career.

When you left the room I assumed that you were not coming back.

I feared that I would lose my equanimity.

This is not Baden; one may not ramble about here, it's forbidden.

It was forbidden for you to enlist in the army! Nevertheless you utterly disregarded my wishes and almost ruined your life—to say nothing of what you did to mine!

Because I took you by the lapels?

I was not thinking of your physical assault upon me. Since, however, we are on the subject, only Oedipus ever dared raise his hand against his father—And bear in mind that you were still my son in June! I opposed you for your own good. From the start my only object has been your welfare—Indeed your welfare and mine are indivisible! But that is something quite beyond your comprehension. Thus you have always judged my actions as stemming from self-interest—Fool! It's you— your judgment which stems from a lack, nay, an abysmal lack of magnanimity and heart-felt love—It's you

I will not have you

Let me finish! My sole request was for you to complete your studies— thereafter you would be free to pursue whatever career you wished— But no! you went ahead in utter disregard

Concerning my enlistment, I

I have not finished! When you reversed your decision, I thought that you had seen the daylight. You yourself confessed that the army is no place for a youth fluent in Greek and Latin, not to mention French and English—After all, I didn't spend tens of thousands on your education for you to become a vulgarian!

I would remind you that I joined the army out of desperation, to free myself from you, I mean from your reproaches. Yet even now, upon reflection, I wish to make it my career.

Alas!—I made my worst mistake last year

Be so good as to come to the point; I'm very tired.

I should never have permitted you to matriculate at the Polytechnic Institute—It was a miserable step down to abandon your studies at the University for a business career, worse still for a military career—Even so, you have until September 3rd to make good your examinations at the Institute.

I shall never go back there, unless of course you insist upon it.

No doubt you fear that you'll fail the examinations a second time.

I fear no such thing! I went to the Institute only because your brother persuaded both of us that I should—Uncle Johann notwithstanding, I'm not suited to a business career.

Nor to music, nor to philology—only to the army

That is unjust; a military career requires as much industry and discipline as any other.

It's useless to argue since I can be of no help to you in that pursuit.

On the contrary, if I'm not mistaken, the officer in charge of the military academy at Neustadt, a certain Colonel Faber, is under the command of your Royal pupil's elder brother.

Let us drop the subject—I will never agree to a military career!

But Uncle

Never—that is final!!!

The priest has come in—I'll introduce you to him, but then you must leave, *without conversation* I beseech you.

Mr. Beethoven, I am honored to meet you.

In all modesty I have had considerable experience in these matters.

Heretofore I have had no difficulty distinguishing between a true and false conversion.

You may rest assured that your nephew will have to apply himself zealously to the task at hand.

———

AUGUST 24, 1826

My dear Stephan,

I urgently need to consult with you. Can you possibly imagine the subject? Right you are—my nephew! Joking aside, if it's not too bothersome, I can stop by this evening either before or after supper, whichever suits you best.

In great haste, your

BEETHOVEN

———

Ludwig, I agreed to let Gerhard receive you providing he returned to his room immediately.

With regard to your nephew what is the latest difficulty?

I would ask you not to dismiss the idea out of hand; in my view the army might be the best place for him.

In that respect all of us are slaves. I am a slave to the War Department, Gerhard is a slave to school, and you yourself, are you not a slave to composition? For your nephew to be a slave to the army might in fact prove beneficial to him; after all, we have seen what freedom brought him.

What better cure for profligacy! The army will bridle the boy in no time.

I do in fact know Colonel Faber.

You are right to assume that your nephew would graduate as an officer. But even so, the military academy is not useful for your purposes. Were you to send him there, his schooling in Vienna would go for nought; he would have to start all over again, to drill and study for years. Surely he is not likely to fall in with such a plan. Besides, you would have to pay for him at Neustadt.

Consider this: I have an acquaintance at the War Department, a certain Lieutenant Field-Marshal Baron von Stutterheim, who commands his own regiment. I shall try to persuade him to grant your nephew a cadetship. If the Baron agrees, the boy would obtain a commission more quickly than at Neustadt and at much less cost to you.

His regiment is stationed in Moravia.

At Iglau.

Two days by coach.

I grant you that Neustadt is nearer, yet the farther he is from Vienna the better. Indeed the distance will strengthen his discipline.

True enough, yet the army will bring to an end more than his boyhood; in some wise, Ludwig, it will also end your fatherhood.

Come quickly, I'll lead the way.

Seeing that you have soiled your linen, we had better stop for now.

Never mind the Lieutenant Field-Marshal, you need not decide the matter to-night.

By all means, if I can. What is the favor?

Won't Holz be serving as your agent there?

In that case what is the need for both of us?

If my presence at the hearing will put you at your ease, rest assured that I'll be there. Please have Holz inform me of the hour.

———

Maestro, Councilor Breuning was in the courtroom from the start.

Your nephew was brought in by the police.

No, he sat in a chair throughout.

Of his behavior in general he said that he became worse because you demanded that he be better.

When Czapka probed his motive, your nephew declared that he was driven not by hatred of you but by other feelings.

For example he—Indeed he mostly voiced the same complaints that you told me were put forward in his letter.

That you reproached him too much.

That you kept him under constant surveillance.

That you held him "imprisoned."

On the contrary, the court acknowledged *all that you have done for him*.

At the same time, however, the court found that if Karl acted in accordance with natural instinct and expressed the wish to live with his mother, it could hardly object.

Please calm yourself, the finding was merely conjectural; your nephew expressed no such wish.

Since he will not be discharged for several weeks it's premature to fret.

But I said that your nephew expressed no such wish, not even the wish to *visit* his mother.

Why do you speak of your brother?

May I read it?

GNEIXENDORF, AUGUST 24, 1826

Dearest Brother,

 I am taking this opportunity to wish you the very best for tomorrow, your name day. During this trying time while Karl is in the hospital and the summer heat is still cooking Vienna (*here* the air grows crisper), I want to invite you yet again to spend some weeks with us. From my former experience as an apothecary I know how much good the change would do you—travel is always good for one's health. God only knows how much healthier, let alone richer, you would be today if you had listened to your little brother last year and gone to London when the Philharmonic Society invited you. But never mind, that is yesterday's chamber pot. (By the by, I hope that there has been no recurrence of the Kolik; in any case please keep in mind that the powders I left for you are in the chest of drawers between the windows.) Surely by now the terms of my invitation are as familiar to you as the nose on your face: I will put at your disposal three very large and beautiful rooms with a grand view of the Danube valley. After the chestnut trees shed their leaves, one can see all the way to Styria! You already know from my numerous gifts how superb the wines of this region are, but you have yet to discover our beef, goose, trout—Even as I write, the spittle is running down my chin!

Time and again you have stated that your only reason for refusing my invitations is your dislike, to put it mildly, of my wife and her daughter. Reconsider, I implore you! For *your* sake I ask you to let bygones be bygones. Before your health fails you utterly, do come here and see my beautiful estate. Therese has all that she can do to supervise the servants and manage the household; thus you will set eyes on her only at the dinner table. As for the daughter, rest assured that Amalie will seldom cross your path. By the by, the girl just turned 19—Imagine! Oh how the years run away! All the more reason then for you to accept my invitation. Providence alone knows the length of time alotted to each of us; although I am four years younger than you, it is conceivable that I could be taken first. On the other hand—But away with such unwholesome thoughts.

> With love and best regards, your most devoted brother
>
> JOHANN

Maestro, have you answered him?

May I read the reply?

VIENNA, AUGUST 28, 1826

I am not coming—

> Your brother??????!!!!
>
> LUDWIG

Maestro, Tacitus himself could not have put it more succinctly.

Try not to dwell on your brother. All that really matters now is whether there will be another quartet.

That is music to my ears—or soon will be. In what key?

But that will be the third one in F. There is still none in D minor.

What has your nephew to do with it?

Come now, I told you that he expressed no such wish. Yet even if he should decide to live with his mother

In all likelihood Breuning is at home; he walked back just ahead of me.

Gladly, I'll wait and take it to him.

My dear Stephan!
    Thank you very much for attending the Inquisition—After weighing the pros and cons, I have decided that I would like you to approach the Lieutenant Field-Marshal—prestissimo! It's much more urgent than I realized when we spoke, so do use all the cunning of Ulysses.

In the greatest haste, your

B.

SEPTEMBER 1, 1826

My dear Ludwig,
    I have good news! The Lieutenant Field-Marshal has agreed to give your nephew a cadetship. Let us confer as soon as possible.

Your devoted friend

STEPHAN

Ludwig, no cunning was required. The Lieutenant Field-Marshal is an admirer of your music; thus he was quick to look with favor upon the proposal. Indeed if your nephew shapes up, Baron von Stutterheim will hold a place for him as an officer.

The plan is as follows: as soon as your nephew is discharged from the hospital

I remembered his hernia operation and gave that as the reason for his being laid up.—As soon as he is discharged, I'll present him to the Lieutenant Field-Marshal. The next day he'll swear the oath of service; thence he must obtain his medical certificate, be fitted for uniforms, equipped with

The whole procedure takes six or seven days.

I suppose that he'll stay with you since you are his guardian.

But he expressed no wish to stay with his mother.

He'll leave for Iglau the moment the uniforms are ready.

It can't be postponed; now that the wheels are set in motion, the plan *must* go forward.

I stepped out because I recognized your rapt expression. You were in one of those reveries which my mother termed a raptus and teased you for when we were young.

I know that such reveries often bear musical ideas, I didn't know they could also bear legal ones.

Pertaining to what?

Seeing that I have been urging you to resign the guardianship for months, I am pleased of course. The decision is both judicious and prudent; moreover it is logical. Once your nephew leaves for Iglau, you will have acquitted yourself of your duty as a father; thereafter no further decisions, at least none of importance, will have to be taken.

All the same there is still one matter unsettled. Since your nephew does not reach his majority until he is 24, a new guardian will have to be appointed.

Whom do you have in mind?

I am honored, naturally. However, in my view Dr. Bach would be a better choice.

Because, as you know, I am not an admirer of your nephew.

Ah! so it's *you* who resorts to the cunning of Ulysses. When you put it that way, how can I refuse?

I laughed at myself, not at you. Ten years ago I frowned on your being his guardian, now I have agreed to be appointed.

Please have Holz inform the Magistrate.

It goes without saying that I would welcome your thoughts on the subject; do jot them down at your leisure.

———

In Karl's case three points should be borne in mind, I think. Firstly, he must not be treated like a convict, for such treatment would not produce the result we desire, but precisely the opposite—secondly, if he is to be promoted to the higher ranks, he must not live too frugally and shabbily—thirdly, he would find it hard to face too great a restriction in eating and drinking—But I do not wish to forestall you.

———

Maestro, Czapka said that he will gladly appoint Breuning as your replacement.

Not only was he quick to agree, but he did so with a smile.

You are forgetting how agitated you were after your last visit to the hospital.

If it's merely a matter of conveying your name day wishes

By all means suit yourself.

———

Uncle, after what happened last time, I told Holz that I didn't want you to visit again.

The Emperor granted me a dispensation for your name day—Well now, I'm heartened to see some color in your cheeks and to find you sitting up and reading the Bible—presumably for the priest. Has he worked your conversion yet?

Indeed he has.

Backward to the Dark Ages?

I, too, was skeptical at first, yet now I begin to be convinced, not by his teachings but by the man himself. He is utterly altruistic and sincere.

How like you to discern those qualities in a mystical priest, yet fail to see them in your Uncle! But never mind, for your name day—Note well that I, unlike a certain thankless party, have not forgotten the occasion—Apropos of the Bible, I bring you glad tidings!

Why are you silent? Am I to guess the tidings?

Certainly not—All arrangements are now in place for a military career.

Thank you, Uncle, a thousand thanks; you have made me very happy.

If so, why do you remove your hand from mine?

How could I otherwise write down my response? Were matters arranged by Colonel Faber?

No, by a friend of Breuning's at the War Department, a certain Lieutenant Field-Marshal von Stutterheim. He has agreed to give you a cadetship in his regiment.

That is even better than the academy, promotion might occur sooner.

Don't be too quick to count chickens.

Where will I be stationed?

In Moravia—which should warm your heart seeing that it takes you so far from your Jailer!

What I wish to be far from is Vienna, which should warm *yours.* May I know what the plan is?

As soon as you are discharged from this dungeon, Breuning will present you to the Lieutenant Field-Marshal. Immediately thereafter—Why do you finger the bandage?

I was thinking of the scar; I fear that it may still be visible after I'm discharged.

Since that is three or four weeks hence, let us lose no sleep—At any rate, while you are waiting for your health certificate and uniforms etc.

you'll stay with me; then as soon as everything is in order, you'll leave for Iglau.

How long shall I be with you?

four or five days

What is the matter, has the cat got your tongue?—In view of the possibility that you may never see me again, are five days too many to spend with your guardian?

Of course not, nor will it be our last time together. Simply because I join von Stutterheim's regiment doesn't mean

And what would you do if I were not your guardian?

I don't understand the question.

Would you still wish to stay with me?

What are you fishing for?

I have decided to resign the guardianship in favor of Councilor Breuning.

Why do you make such a face?

Again the cat!

Breuning doesn't like me.

Tant pis! perhaps now you'll come to appreciate your former guardian's devotion. Well, what shall I tell the Councilor—are you or are you not in agreement with the plan?

I am, naturally.

———

Maestro, I'll thank you to stop saying "old married man"; I have been in the blissful state but a scant five days. As for procreating, I can only tell you that I apply myself assiduously and with Catullan ardor.

Concerning your nephew, I'm afraid there is an unforeseen development.

No need for me to do so, he has explained the matter himself.

SEPTEMBER 18, 1826

Dear Uncle,

Now that the bandages have been removed the worst is upon us: where the bullet entered the flesh a void stands out as hairless as limestone. Under the circumstances I cannot possibly be presented to the Lieutenant Field-Marshal, not until all sign of what happened is covered over.

Your dutiful nephew

KARL

Maestro, that would indeed make sense, were it not that your nephew has changed his mind.

He is no longer willing to stay with you.

Please don't excite yourself, not a word was said about staying with his mother.

Evidently the priest is satisfied; thus Dr. Seng intends to discharge him a week from today.

Unquestionably, but the trick is how to persuade your nephew.

In my opinion Breuning ought to visit the hospital tomorrow, not only to find out why your nephew changed his mind, but to remind him in plain words of the promise he made you.

———

Ludwig, your nephew will go wherever I deem best. At the same time he asked me, as his newly appointed guardian, not to make him come back here.

If only to forestall a repetition of what happened in July, I venture to say that I agree with him.

His reason, which I must say I find convincing: if he were here, you would have too much to say to him and that would cause new quarrels.

That is water under the bridge. Now the salient question is what would be best *for both of you*.

In truth he expressed a preference to stay with his mother.

Your nephew is now 20 years old. No matter how depraved his mother is, she cannot be held responsible forever for his actions.

At his age he is sure to encounter such women wherever he goes, not solely at his mother's.

Then let him stay with *me*.

If he runs away, he will run away wherever I send him.

In that case perhaps you should speak to him yourself.

———

Uncle, since it's such a beautiful day the Sister permitted me sit in the garden.

After so many weeks of confinement, the moment I stepped out of doors I found myself singing your Prisoners' Chorus, "Oh, what joy to breathe the scent of open air."

That was kind of Councilor Breuning, but I told him that I wish to stay with my mother.

Back to my room.

Because I will not be upbraided.

Very well, but only on condition that you refrain from such remarks; in no wise have I given you reason to censure me.

Indeed you did say that I was to stay with you, yet for my part I made no such promise.

On the contrary I believe that the Councilor agrees with me.

I won't hear anything derogatory about my mother; it's not for me to judge her. The least I can do to repay her for all she has suffered on my account is to spend that time with her.

Since it's only a matter of four or five days, it makes no sense to speak of a harmful influence on me.

By no means will I treat her more coldly than has been my practice in the past.

All the less reason then to deny her wish to be with me, inasmuch as I'm not likely to be in Vienna soon again.

I fail to see how my staying with her will keep me from being with you.

Rest assured that I'll visit you as often as you like.

Most honorable Magistrate von Czapka,
    I urgently request

Sir!

I urgently request you to arrange that my nephew, who will have recovered in a few days, shall not leave the hospital with anybody but *myself and Mr. Holz*—It is out of the question to allow him to be much in the company of his mother, that extremely depraved person. My anxieties and my request are warranted by her most evil, wicked and spiteful character; her enticement of Karl for the purpose of getting money out of me; the probability that she has spent those sums on him; and that she too is intimate with Karl's dissolute companion Niemetz; the sensation she has been causing with her daughter, *whose father is still being traced*; and, what is more, the likelihood that in his mother's home he would make the acquaintance of women who are anything but virtuous. Even the habit of being in the company of such a person cannot possibly lead a young man along the path of virtue—While asking you to give this matter your most serious consideration I send you my best regards. I merely add the remark that, although the occasion was a painful one, it has given me very great pleasure to have made the acquaintance of a man of such excellent intellectual and moral qualities—

I remain, Sir, with due respect, yours sincerely,
BEETHOVEN

No, Maestro, I'm not early but please don't fret. If you haven't finished, Haslinger will just have to wait. This won't be the first time nor, I suspect, the last that you keep your publisher waiting. One cannot finish the dedication page of one's greatest symphony, compose a letter to the Magistrate and deal with one's brother all in the same breath.

If Czapka has already summoned Breuning, rest assured that your letter hit the mark. As for the manuscript, the delay is entirely the Royal Librarian's fault; he should not have insisted that the corrections be made in your own hand.

Don't misunderstand me, your hand is perfectly legible. And don't concern yourself about the smudges, the bookbinder will clean them up.

The man gives his word that it will be bound handsomely and ready for you next Tuesday, the 26th.

Since the Royal Librarian doesn't return to Berlin until the 29th, there is sufficient time. Altogether the Prussian King should be extremely pleased.

Unfortunately I must return to the office at once. However, on my way here I encountered your brother.

Indeed not, he was riding about in his carriage, with two tricked up servants on the box. Thus he could easily deliver the manuscript to Haslinger and at the same time fetch the Clementi for Gerhard.

By the way your brother said to tell you that he'll be late. The poor man seemed extremely anxious and harried.

Presumably with regard to his property taxes which, he let on, are due on the last day of the month.

I must leave now; do let me know what Breuning reports.

———

Brother, the dedication page is comme il faut—fit for a king, as the saying goes—All joking aside, will you not also write a dedicatory letter to His Majesty?

When I consider that the late father of this Prussian King is sometimes spoken of, behind the hand naturally, as *your own*, I'm at a loss for words. Just imagine! Were the consanguinity true, you and the dedicatee would be half brothers.

If it dishonors the memory of our mother, you could easily deny it, as I and others have urged you to do, yet you insist upon remaining silent—I can't help but think that you take some satisfaction from such gossip.

If your unwillingness to say a word about yourself is a matter of principle, I have no choice but to bow to your silence—indeed it makes your silence golden!

Then let us change the subject—I'm surprised to find so many mistakes in the manuscript; obviously the copyist is an arch-bungler!

It's the same in every trade—unless one does the job oneself, mistakes crop up like crab grass.

Why bring it to the publisher on foot when my carriage-and-four is waiting below?

In that case I'll bring it to Haslinger for you—But first, with regard to this Karl business

Our sister-in-law has been in touch with me.

By no means are we entering into any kind of conspiracy.

Believe me, I am not siding with Johanna—on the contrary

If only you would listen, I have a proposal to make—Since you are opposed to his staying with his mother, and Breuning is opposed to his staying here with you, what better plan than for you to come to Gneixendorf—the two of you, en famille. It would surely do you a world of good. Anyone can see that you haven't fully recovered from your last attack of Kolik, to say nothing of what happened with our nephew.

I beg you not to dismiss the idea out of hand.

Come now, you exaggerate my wife's iniquities.

The daughter was too young at the time to know any better.

Even so, what is there to lose?

But *I* will bear all the expenses.

Won't you at least

Calm yourself, I'm on my way to Haslinger presto!

———

Thank you, Ludwig, Gerhard will be overjoyed. From the moment that you mentioned the Clementi the boy has not stopped chattering about the book. Now he will have no further excuse to put off practicing.

As to Czapka, I am afraid that his ruling will satisfy neither you nor your sister-in-law; indeed it makes your brother's invitation seem all but providential.

In brief, upon discharge from the hospital your nephew is ordered to spend the following fortnight *outside of Vienna*.

When I asked if the ruling permitted him to go to Hetzendorf or Döbling etc., Czapka declared that "any and all environs" were forbidden.

Because that is how long I assumed it would take for the hair to grow back in. Thus I told Czapka and, I may say, with a bit of Ulyssean cunning, that your nephew is obliged to join his regiment in two weeks' time.

The ruling strikes me as judicious; not only does it remove him from the chance of familial strife, but from the temptations of Vienna.

I did not mean—I was thinking only of billiards and gambling.

I am concealing *nothing*. If your nephew has a mistress, I know nothing of it.

The name of Niemetz is unfamiliar to me; what is more, I consider such an attachment unlikely.

Suspicion aside, let us determine where he is to go.

I have no idea; perhaps Czapka assumed he would go directly to his regiment, but that is out of the question. With whom would he stay at Iglau? Or indeed elsewhere?

In fact there is no other possibility, which is why your brother's invitation comes as such a godsend.

How much harm could the woman do in two weeks' time?

I know you, Ludwig; once you decide to go to Gneixendorf you'll find a way to stomach your sister-in-law. You have done so in the past and can do so again—It's all *in the deciding*.

Thank goodness; at times you run Prince Hamlet a close race. Now we must inform your nephew.

It's no imposition, I could easily stop at the hospital tomorrow. But would it not be wiser to tell him yourself or, better still, to go there with your brother? In that way your nephew won't hold you alone responsible for the decision.

———

But Uncle, what I fail to understand, and in this Uncle Johann agrees with me, is why we don't set out on Tuesday. If Czapka forbids me to be here after Monday, he'll surely not allow me to stay two or three days more while the bookbinder binds the score.

You could write the dedicatory letter to H.M. beforehand.

Holz could bring it to the Royal Librarian for you.

Brother, my business cannot wait on so many ifs, ands and buts—I must be back in Gneixendorf by Friday at the latest.

Clearly you are forgetting the overnight stop in St. Polten—even if we set out at the crack of dawn on Wednesday

Uncle, in that case I'll tell my mother to expect me on Monday!

I understand that I'm not to leave the hospital with anyone but you or Holz; however, if you intend to flout the ruling, I don't see why

Brother, don't be so quick to cry conspiracy—I merely told our nephew that we are wasting time bickering over what amounts to one day. Further, I suggested that it would be truly unkind of him to stay with his mother for so brief a period, since it would only serve to tantalize the poor woman.

I'm happy to say that our nephew bows to my greater wisdom. Thus our departure is now in the hands of the gods—or, to be exact, of the bookbinder.

———

Maestro, you are overhasty. Far be it from me to instruct you in the laws of nature, yet generally these matters take nine months.

Dr. Seng expects us to come for your nephew at one o'clock; hence Sali plans to serve at two. She showed me the carp, it's a beauty!

If you think it will smooth the waters with Karl, I'll be glad to join you for dinner. I'll tell Sali on my way out.

Although the bookbinder assures me he hasn't slept or eaten in three days, he no longer promises you'll have the manuscript tomorrow.

Not until Wednesday—with luck.

I'll simply inform His Royal Librarianship that there has been a slight delay.

Why do you assume that the Royal Librarian smokes cigarros?

That's a different matter; of course I know that your nephew enjoys them. I'll fetch some on my way to work. And don't forget that Gerhard will be coming here from school; according to Breuning the boy is quite taken with the Clementi.

———

Prospero, thank you so much for Clementi's *System*; I'm most honored by the interest you take in my playing.

In all concience I would have to admit that my fingering is not perfect.

Oh dear, I always have difficulty with *sc* words. Would you like to see my fingering?

I didn't realize that you were watching for expression; I was concentrating on the fingering. In future I'll use more pedal.

Most likely I won't see you again before you leave for Gneixendorf.

It's not a stroke of luck; with Gneixendorf I made certain beforehand to find out the spelling.

By the time you return there should be a ~~noticea~~ a good deal of improvement in my playing; I plan to practice every day.

I must go now, otherwise I'll be late for dinner. I hope that you have a safe journey and a pleasing two weeks with your brother.

———

Uncle, many thanks for the cigarros. Only now does it begin to dawn on me that I have left the hospital. Just imagine, a cigarro after dinner! And what a dinner! You are right to say that your Sali is the first good cook you

Because I don't regard her as *mine*.

But I don't regard this apartment as mine, I mean as my home.

You are wrong to assume anything of the kind; my mother's place is *her's.* It so happens that I have no home at present, unless it be at Iglau.

Maestro, forgive me but I must go back to my work now.

Indeed I did. What is more, I told the man that you'll bind him hand and foot with his very own binding cord if he fails you on Wednesday. Meanwhile don't forget that you must still compose the dedicatory letter to H.M.

I'll let myself out.

Uncle, I don't wish to appear ungrateful, but if we are to leave on Wednesday, I too have a million things to attend to.

At dinner you said that the letter must be in your own hand.

In that case why ask

Very well, I'll help you draft it, providing that you know more or less what you wish to say. But do let's be quick about it.

Your Majesty!

One of the great happinesses of my life is that Your Majesty has most graciously permitted me to dedicate the present work to you in all humility.

Your Majesty is not only the supreme father of your subjects but also the patron of arts and sciences. How much more, therefore, must your most gracious permission delight me, seeing that I too, since I am a native of Bonn, am fortunate enough to regard myself as one of your subjects.

I request Your Majesty most graciously to accept this work as a slight indication of the high regard I cherish for your supreme virtues—Your Majesty's most humble and most obedient

LUDWIG VAN BEETHOVEN

———

Maestro, the bookbinder has failed us! He now says that he will have it tomorrow.

There is *nothing* to do about it except to resume your seat and finish your porridge. Everything, including your brother's property taxes, will simply have to wait a day.

Your brother is not late, I am early.

Your nephew assured me that he would apply himself this morning to the metronome markings.

That must be your brother now.

Brother, I can see that for myself—your face is blood red. What excuse did the scoundrel

But surely Czapka won't grant you

Never mind H.M., if we don't depart the day after tomorrow, I'll be ruined!

Heavens no, that would be too dear—Why, for you to follow in a hired carriage would cost you a pretty penny.

Congratulations! However, a "token" from a monarch might turn out a mere souvenir or, God grant, a castle. What sort of token has H.M. hinted at?

Well and good, yet there is a world of difference between a decoration and something costly.

Although the Royal Order of the Red Eagle, Second Class, is nothing to sneeze at, it won't pay your way to Gneixendorf. Call me what you will—neither one of us is so well off that he can thumb his nose at costly things. I'll be curious to learn what Ambassador Hatzfeld reports.

Maestro, I told your brother that it wasn't Hatzfeld but the Royal Librarian Spiker who will be coming here.

Let's not waste time; I'll go to the Prussian Embassy at once to postpone the meeting.

I'll try to arrange it for the same hour tomorrow.

Maestro Beethoven, your enthusiasm does H.M. full justice. He is indeed a modern Medici, although neither Cosimo nor Lorenzo had dedicated to *him* a great symphony with choruses.

I cannot speak for the All-Highest; for myself I find the dedication, to say nothing of the letter, altogether praiseworthy.

I do not quite follow you.

Ah! I failed to grasp the pun. Notwithstanding the form, the worth of praise derives from the worth of its author.

Suffice it to say that H.M. regards you with favor.

If by praise in its material form you are alluding to the Royal Order of the Red Eagle, Second Class, such talk may prove more than idle gossip.

Kindly stop there; beyond that point silence, nay, the strictest silence reigns.

You may depend upon me to transmit the score as safely and swiftly—or, better still, mercurially—as the messenger of the gods.

True enough, yet Mercury was an infant when he stole the cows. Rest assured that I am much too old and loyal to H.M. to carry off your great symphony.

———

Frankly, Brother, if I were you I wouldn't wish to stake my hopes on something that may—ergo may *not*—prove more than idle gossip.

Maestro, there isn't the slightest doubt that you'll receive the decoration; the only question is when.

Uncle, it surely makes no difference one way or the other; you will not be a greater man with the decoration than you are now without it.

Brother, decoration or no decoration I'll call for you up at 5 o'clock tomorrow morning. Kindly be downstairs without delay.

Come now, it's not as if we don't receive the post in Lower Austria; you'll have plenty of time to finish your correspondence there.

Well and good, but do be downstairs at 5 sharp!

———

Gentlemen!

As I am just about to go off to the country, I inform you in great haste that you will soon receive the metronome markings of the symphony.

I hope that you have now received the C sharp minor quartet. Don't be frightened at the four sharps. This work will shortly be performed in Vienna for the benefit of an artist.

Finally I must request

Brother, it is now 5:04—I've been waiting seven minutes! Yet lo and behold, what do I find? Instead of taking down the bags, our nephew sits here taking down a letter!

Spare me please—If you are not downstairs in exactly three minutes, you may walk to Gneixendorf.

I pointed out a mistake to your amanuensis: today is the 28th not the 29th—Thank God! or I would be undone. Do make haste!

you to hasten the necessary preliminaries connected with the publication of my collected works. I really cannot conceal from you the fact that if I did not keep my promises so honorably, you might easily find yourself at a disadvantage on account of proposals which other publishers have made to me on this subject.

Hoping to hear from you about this very soon, your devoted

BEETHOVEN

3

BROTHER, did I exaggerate? Are these rooms not spacious and grand? Of course they are no match for certain palaces in town, yet for a manor house in Gneixendorf, a village so small that we are obliged to post our letters at Krems, are they not passable?

And this sitting room, is it not a choice spot in which to work on your quartets?

They face south to the Danube, while those on your left face east. The ruins in the distance are of Grafenegg Castle—it's fitted up with a moat. Once all the baggage has been brought in, we'll step outside and I'll show you our glorious views.

I told Karl to instruct the boy as to which bags belong in here and which in the bedroom and dressing room—By the way, the boy's name is Michael; he is just short of sixteen and a most agreeable lad. My wife has ordered him to look after your needs—In town Michael would be designated a valet, here he is merely a servant.

Naturally, that is why Therese chose him. But question him yourself.

Michael, do you read and write?

Yes, Master Brother, Michael read and write.

And how are you with numbers?

Has the cat got your tongue?

Michael must use fingers.

Frankly, so must I!

Brother, your smile suggests that my wife has done well—Ah! speak of the mistress and she appears.

Brother-in-law, I bid you welcome.

Don't say such things, even in jest. On the contrary gentians are medicinal; they are meant to prolong life, not to decorate a grave. My sole object in collecting the nosegay was to wish you a most healthy and comfortable stay.

If you should want for anything—apart from wood which I have already made certain is in ample store; but should you need linens or laundering or to have your razor sharpened or your boots blackened, I have chosen a hard-working lad

I'm pleased that he already meets with your approval.

The piano is in the salon. We considered bringing it up here. Since, however, you are staying but two weeks and the salon is so nearby— it's just to the right at the foot of the stairs.

I do hope that you remembered to bring the pieces for four hands; I've been practicing at every opportunity.

Why, for us to play together, should you be so inclined.

I certainly don't wish to appear presumptuous. Indeed I know how poorly I play—only your brother plays worse than I do.

And now if you'll excuse me, I must see to supper.

I'm sorry to hear that. Was it something you ate last night at the inn?

In that case the best thing would be broth with rice and bread with goat cheese. I'll go and tell the cook.

Brother, seeing that we still have a good deal of time before supper, I'll now show you some of our breath-taking views.

Hardly, we would need the better part of a day to see the whole estate—keep in mind that it's 400 acres! Why, even the vineyard will have to wait until tomorrow.

For now we'll restrict ourselves to the gardens and fields. I especially want you to see our magnificent view of the valley. Who knows, it may even be clear enough today to see—Ah! but why spoil it? I'll let that remain a surprise—Come, we'll fetch Karl.

He must be unpacking. His room is just beyond these at the end of the passage.

No, ours are on the other side of the house. You'll see them another time.

————

Uncle, of course I remembered. Not only did I bring pieces by Clementi and Haydn, etc., but also Lannoy's Marches; they are in the tan portmanteau beside

I don't follow you. Are you suggesting that I play four hands with Aunt Therese?

But I brought them in order to accompany *you*; surely that was your object in

Brother, if we don't set out soon, we'll see nothing but the dusk.

———

Brother, I grant you that the land is "flat" and "bald" and all the rest of it, yet tell me if you've ever seen the equal of this prospect.

The Danube, naturally!

Hardly a village, that is Krems—we'll visit it tomorrow.

That is the surprise I mentioned earlier. Come, venture a guess—where do you suppose those mountains are situated?

Even though you spoke in jest, you are not far off the mark—Styria!

Well, there you are—the view from Olympus! The rest of our wonders will have to wait until tomorrow. Let's go back now and wash up—supper is served at 7:30.

———

Uncle, it's utterly unjust of you to blame Breuning; he had no way of knowing that there are no trees in Gneixendorf. Besides, since there was no other place for us, we would have come here in any case.

Thus far the hospitality of your brother, not to mention Fat Stuff, has been exemplary; your rooms are surprisingly comfortable, the servant is to your liking—All that remains is the food; and that, needless to say, can't be judged on the merit of rice soup. Have you any appetite whatever?

Then let us go downstairs, it's 7:25.

Brother-in-law, before you retire, at what hour do you take your hot water in the morning?

Don't be concerned about the servant, surely it's his job to accommodate you.

In that case I'll have him leave it for you in the sitting room at 5:30; breakfast is served at 7:30. Does that suit you?

Considering your bowels, perhaps you should take a cup of chocolate instead of coffee with breakfast.

I don't see why you shouldn't, porridge can't possibly harm you.

Do have a restful night.

Uncle, most of the table talk concerned the journey. Firstly your brother boasted of our speed in reaching St. Polten; then he complained of the meat salad, the mattress, the exorbitant charges, etc. When Fat Stuff spoke it was only to inquire about your comfort and to note what foods would be best for you under the circumstances.

As for Little Bastard, she spoke but once: to ask her mother's permission to remove her stole.

Perhaps the time has come to change your epithet for Amalie to Slut; after all, she is far from *little* at present.

I agree that she comes by it honestly, although the mother-whore knows better than to flaunt her bare shoulders and bosom at table.

Only the soprano Milder has bigger ones than Slut.

Apart from being overfed and spoiled, I find her disagreeable. She pouts too much; worse still, she looks down her nose at the servants, especially at Michael.

Presumably he serves at every meal; he'll tell you in the morning when he brings the hot water.

Should you happen to be working, he has been instructed not to disturb you.

How soon do you expect to finish the new quartet?

In that case you would do well to go to bed forthwith; you scarcely slept at all last night.

Master Brother, excuse disturb work.

Woman with Michael cook. Cook do bed, Michael mop.

After breakfast? But Mistress say

Michael go tell cook, then come back.

No, Michael never see such mark.

Michael understand, not touch cortet.

Michael, the word is written quartet.

Not touch quartet or paper or pencil or

Anything, Michael understand, not touch anything on table.

Or anywhere else.

At what hour Michael come back?

Michael understand, every day clean bedroom 5:30, this one wait until 8:30 after Master Brother go for walk.

Cook say bed finish now. Michael come back after breakfast when Master Brother go to vineyard.

———

Brother, I crushed the grapes in my palm to determine the stickiness of the juice. At this moment the sugar is all but perfect. Thus they are virtually ready for harvest.

Sometime next week, you'll know which day it is from the zealous activity hereabouts.

After the grapes are picked and crushed, mostly by sundown, I give the workers *gratis* as much wine as they can drink—with the predictable result of a nightlong saturnalia.

Payment indeed! the wine they guzzle is sufficient payment—The rest I sell to a vintner in Krems.

The grapes are Rheinriesling, naturally—the finest in the region.

Spare me! That is hardly a blemish—On the contrary the speckles you see are their mark of distinction. Do taste one.

Is it not ambrosia?—Excuse me a moment.

It's de rigueur—all my tenants bow to me. I had to bring the man's attention to a vine which needed trimming—A penny saved is a penny earned, as the saying goes—especially today with my taxes due.

Well now, to work—you to the fields, I to confer with my steward. Dinner is at 12:30.

Tant pis! In the Waldviertel you'll find trees, here we have only fields. Frankly I don't see what difference it makes since your walks are taken not for recreation but to stimulate composition.

I don't pretend to know whence inspiration comes, whether from trees or Providence; still, there is no reason to suppose that your muse will abandon you in Gneixendorf. You'll see quite enough trees this afternoon on the way to Krems. I've ordered the carriage for 1:15.

—————

Uncle, there is more to see in Krems than I expected.

This is the Dominican church that Uncle Johann mentioned; it's now used as a theater.

He said it had just opened this June with a performance of *Intrigue and Love*.

There is still plenty of time to look at the shops before we are due to meet him.

Why do you stop here?

But there is nothing special about this Plague-column; like all the rest in Austria it simply commemorates those who died in 1679.

Even so, you pass the one in town almost daily without so much as a glance. Why does this one command your attention?

Come now, don't slip into a morbid humor; the Plague is long since over.

I'll thank you not to say another word about my mother.

Then let us go on to the stationer's.

———

Uncle, here quills are 15 kreuzer less than in town.

Sealing wax and pencils are virtually the same, but notebooks are dearer.

1 gulden 20 kreuzer

I'm afraid that is not a good idea.

I don't mean that we shouldn't set out for the coffee house, although we are still early for your brother, but that you shouldn't drink coffee; you would do well to take chocolate instead.

The stationer says that if we go to the far end of the street and turn left at the church, we cannot miss it.

———

Uncle, please don't speak so loudly; since we are strangers here everyone is curious to have a look at us and listen to our conversation.

It was your brother who chose this place, not I. Besides, it's not nearly so wicked as you suggest. Perhaps the Plague-column is still weighing upon your mind.

Because I take an interest in the billiard players doesn't mean that I wish to gamble, nor that I take no interest in what you are saying.

First of all you said that I should be mindful of my health; secondly, that I should do nothing to enfeeble my youthful vigor; thirdly, that sensual gratification without spiritual union is bestial; and fourthly, that I should eschew the company of plague-ridden whores.

Rest assured that I plan to keep out of harm's way during—Here now is your brother.

By no means, Brother, I'm just putting a face on it for those busybodies over there, especially that swine with spectacles—In truth I'm ready to collapse.

The filthy vulture picked me clean!

Not the bespectacled swine, *the tax collector*. As usual I'm left with nothing but bare bones! Thank God the month is over—perhaps things will improve with the harvest.

Alas, I have no appetite. We should start back in any case, it's late—Come, pay your bill, I can't afford to treat you.

Now, now, I was only joshing—For Heaven's sake don't let us have a scene.

———

Master Brother, Michael not know why cook laugh at you.

Cook should not come back?

Never come back?

Michael not come back?

Michael now mop and clean and also do bed, Michael understand, tell Mistress.

Not tell Mistress?

They are 20 kreutzer piece.

They are 3.

For Michael? Not understand.

Gift?

Thank you Master Brother, thank you very much!

Must Michael tell Mistress of gift?

If Michael laugh like cook, must give back gift?

Michael not know why cook laugh. Perhaps—Michael not know.

Perhaps cook laugh because Master Brother stamp feet and pound table and sing when write quartet.

Yes, march at school.

Yes, dance but not good.

rithum?

Michael, the word is written rhythm.

Please write new word for Michael.

That is termed measure.

Why 6 above 8?

One reads the numbers as if they were written—6/8, 3/4, 2/4, etc, to show the beat of the rhythm which is termed time.

How write time?

*Just as you have done—*time.

Beating time?

Tomorrow when Michael hear Master Brother stamp feet, Michael understand beating time.

Mostly Michael finish work after supper.

Come back here then, tell Master Brother what Master and Mistress and Daughter and Son say at supper?

Dinner too? How remember from noon to night what say?

Yes Michael remember. Yesterday Master Brother tell Michael tell Mistress bowel better, eat same food family eat at dinner.

Master Brother trick Michael.

But Michael not remember everything.

Very well, Michael try, come back after supper.

———

GNEIXENDORF, OCTOBER 2, 1826

Chief of all Tobiases!

There is no time left today for the remaining consonant-tizings and vocalizings. But please deliver the enclosed letter at once.

I know you will forgive me for troubling you. But since you are now the proprietor of an art post office, well, naturally we cannot help making use of it.

You see that I am here in Gneixendorf. The name resembles to a certain extent a breaking axle. The air is healthy. As to everything else one must cross oneself and say Memento Mori.

Your most devoted

BEETHOVEN

Uncle, I have left space to insert the musical setting for Haslinger.

Do you wish it to be in your hand or mine?

Since you ask, the remarks about Gneixendorf strike me as unjust.

"Everything else" includes the rooms, your brother, Fat Stuff, Michael

What objection have you to the food? After all, it was only last night that you resumed eating the regular fare, and today for your first dinner she served you goose.

With goose one always goes a little hungry, yet one doesn't always remark on it to one's hostess.

In that regard you are wrong; she left the table not in anger but to tell the cook to prepare you some Bratwurst. It wouldn't do, she said, to have "the greatest composer of the age" starve to death at Gneixendorf.

The dish failed to appear only because your brother forbade her to give the order. He then quoted the old saw: hungry at bedtime, hearty at dawn.

Perhaps if he were charging you room and board, you might request roast beef, but hardly as his guest.

My shoulder?

But I felt nothing. Are you certain?

If indeed Fat Stuff touched me on the shoulder before resuming her seat, I am completely unaware of it.

To post the letters. Are we not finished?

At Krems, naturally, since I cannot post them here.

Rest assured that there is scarcely time to walk to Krems and back, let alone to play at billiards.

———

Master Brother, when you say still hungry, Mistress say she order Bratwurst.

Son say Mistress not fret, Master Brother not starve.

Never hear Mistress and Son say thou and thee.

Sometime Mistress say Karl for Son, sometime Son say Aunt for Mistress.

Not see Mistress come back to table. Michael mostly listen not look.

At supper no one mention goose, mostly grape harvest.

Master say harvest this week.

Thursday.

Beside harvest Master say how much new coach spring cost, how much fix harness, how much blacksmith, how much

Mistress say how much Master Brother cost.

Master Brother angry with Michael?

With Mistress, Michael understand.

Michael also surprise how much Michael remember.

Master Brother wish report *every* night?

But so much left out.

Left out Master say daughter of tenant give birth today.

Again Master Brother trick Michael.

Naturally Michael not forget gift—From now on Michael report every night.

Master Brother, today harvest. Please grant Michael favor.

Please excuse Michael one time not report tonight. At sundown all go to vintner in Krems.

Celebrate harvest.

Eating and drinking and firework.

Yes singing and dancing, naturally.

Yes teasing girls.

Sometimes put snake down dress.

Yes other pranks.

Forget now.

Other boy, not Michael.

Michael no girl friend.

Michael tell truth.

Cannot help blush.

Many thanks for favor.

Even with favor Michael must report after dinner?

Dinner today too many people, not listen well.

Not only family but all harvester.

Not in dining room, outside at big table. Not hear what Master and Mistress and

Cattle? No cattle near table.

Too many people together, Michael understand.

Master Brother not eat with cattle, eat in room. Michael go tell Mistress.

———

Brother-in-law, I would be more than pleased to have Michael serve you in your rooms, were it not that he is obliged to serve twenty-two harvesters, a dozen brats, the five of us and three or four bigwigs who always show up uninvited.

Certainly not, under no circumstances will I hear of your foregoing dinner, especially today when I myself have prepared a dish for you that I hear you cannot live without.

Tenderloin of beef!

A little birdy told me.

Very well, if you insist it was your nephew.

On the contrary, his only object in telling me was to satisfy *you*.

Please don't make so much of it.

Frankly I haven't time to argue; I'll instruct Michael to bring you yours the moment he has finished serving the harvesters.

No, no, it's settled—Bon appetit!

Yes Master Brother, beef ragout.

Why Mistress call ragout tenderloin?

So many people, Mistress serve cheap wine.

Michael fetch coffee?

Good wine under lock and key.

After meal Master Brother watch harvest?

Must finish quartet, Michael understand.

Mistress too busy, not pick grape.

Daughter not pick, stamp.

Daughter pull up dress.

Otherwise dress stain.

Michael not look.

Not see anything.

Cannot help blush.

Daughter pull up dress to knee.

Again Master Brother trick Michael.

Son not pick, only look.

Tell Son come here 3 o'clock, Michael understand.

———

"Darling, why didn't you come to meet me in the vineyard today?"

Uncle, you have forgotten your Goethe; it's from *Roman Elegies*.

To celebrate the harvest I may have taken a drop more than I usually do.

None of that formaldehyde for me; I filled my glass in the house.

Rest assured that I have no special influence with the mistress.—I would like you to come with me now up to the vineyard.

Because you'll find it entertaining.

Indeed that is so, but how did you hear of it already?

Spies even here? I've not seen Holz in Gneixendorf.

Well, whoever it was, he spoke the truth. Customarily the women pick while the men tread, but in Slut's case she suddenly hitched up her skirts and climbed into the wine tub. Needless to say, she caused quite a stir.

On the contrary her avoirdupois served her well: she brought forth every precious drop, so to speak. What is more, even as she labored mightily, Slut applied herself con brio to singing saucy harvest songs. Believe me, it was better than any marionnette show in town.

I haven't spoken of the mother, inasmuch as the mother wasn't in the vineyard this morning. However, she is there now and picking with the others.

By no means did I mention the beef in a spirit of intrigue but simply in answer to her query. Fat Stuff asks me all but daily what dishes will please you most.

She said nothing of going to Krems tonight; this is the first I hear of it.

If the others go, I'll go too.

For no other reason than that I need the recreation; there is too little amusement here.

Seeing that certain players cannot bear to lose, a game of cards is not that enjoyable.—Have you any objection to my going?

In that case I'll tag along with them.

———

Brother, would you believe that a fortnight has passed since your arrival?

Tempus fugit—Thus it behooves you to decide now whether you plan to remain with us.

Everyone has gone to Krems.

My wife went with them—she wished to keep an eye on her daughter.

I trust that you enjoyed the soup.

I heard you the first time, naturally. However, I was waiting for the cook to finish serving and shut the door—the old witch eavesdrops. In answer to your question I have no need to keep an eye on my wife.

You are dwelling on bygones—the dalliance of which you speak occurred three years ago.

That she took a lover is indisputable; that she received him in the house while I lay gravely ill is best forgotten.

Whether the man fucked her three times or four is beside the point —What matters is that my wife surrendered her marriage contract afterwards and entered into an agreement which, as you know, permits me to throw her out the instant she takes up with anyone else.

But there has been no one since. Therese is now 52 years old—my own age, to be sure. Alas, there comes a time when the connubial appetite, let alone its means of expression, shrinks!

Confound that cook! Note the shadow under the door—the witch is still listening! Since we are speaking of my wife, etc., please write your part henceforth.

If only you would throw her out, I would gladly stay in Gneixendorf.

Although she isn't the best cook in the world, she is a hardworker.

I'm speaking of your wife!

But my wife has done nothing to warrant such treatment.

Better still, throw them both out, she and her big-bosomed bastard.

I fail to see how Amalie

Brother, imagine how blissful it would be with just the three of us —you, me and Karl! At 52 there are more pressing things to think about than one's shrinking member. When your time comes, do you wish to give up the ghost in the hands of a woman as depraved as your wife?

Come now, I'm not about to give up the ghost, thanks be to God! Indeed it's *you* who suffers from poor health. In whose hands will you be, my worthy brother?

In Karl's naturally!

Karl will be in the army.

Perhaps

Don't be so mysterious.

Have you noticed his scar of late?

Although I have but one good eye, I'd have to be blind in both to miss it.

Well, perhaps the hair will never grow in.

Perhaps not, but it will surely *overgrow* the scar.

Who knows—However, until it does we must stay here.

Then let us put aside my wife whom you encounter, after all, only at table.—It's obvious from the progress of the quartet that you work well here—with or without trees! You have a fondness for Michael, the food is better than you acknowledge, your health has improved—In short Gneixendorf is a veritable paradise for you. Moreover in light of our nephew's hair—Why, what choice have you but to stay? You must.

"Must it be?"

"It must be."

So be it.

Still, I need hardly remind you that you were invited for only a fort-night. If you now wish to stay longer—Well, as much as I would like to keep you as a guest, frankly I can't afford it.

Never mind, I need no charity from you—thank God!

Believe me, I would gladly do a good deal more were I not so hard pressed for taxes.

Please, spare me the lamentabile.

In that case I'll not mince words—If you wish to live with us, you can have everything for 40 gulden.

A fortnight!

What do you take me for—a *month*, of course.

Swindler!

Don't be asinine—I'll see no profit from it, not a penny! Why, the wood alone

What wood! Your wife stints me! The room in which I work is like an ice-cellar—I'm forever on the verge of chilblains there.

Come now, you exaggerate. In any case it's a good deal warmer here in spring and summer—Besides, if you stay eight months you won't need such capacious quarters.

And if I tug on the corset strings and squeeze myself into smaller quar-

ters—nay, into one miserable servant's room, how much will you charge me?

500 gulden per anum

Bloodsucker!!!

Calm yourself lest you have a stroke like our worthy grandfather— Since arithmetic was never your strong suit, I'll reckon it for you— 40 gulden a month amounts to 500 gulden per anum; that is only *half your pension*—So where, pray tell, is the bloodsucking?

You said eight months, not a year.

Let's not haggle; I'll do whatever pleases you. Indeed there is no rush—take your time and think it over.

In truth I'll think of nothing until I finish the quartet.

———

GNEIXENDORF, OCTOBER 13, 1826

My dear Stephan,

We are writing to you from Signor Fratello's freezing fortress.

My last quartet, the one for Schlesinger, is now finished. What trouble it gave me! I was so indescisive, perhaps because I was thinking of a more far-reaching work, but whatever the reason I simply could not bring myself to compose the last movement. Accordingly, I have given it a title, *The hard-won decision*; and a motto stands at the head, *Must it be?—It must be!* The 80 ducats due me will come in handy, seeing that brother Skinflint is lurking in the wings with outstretched palm. Meanwhile, I must find a copyist and get to work on the new finale for the B flat quartet.

Our reason for staying on a little longer is the lovely weather and the fact that Karl's scar is still quite visible. However, I would not want the Field-Marshal to forget his promise of a cadetship, so please remind him of it, but cunningly.

I shall see you very soon. May God bless you.

With love, your

LUDWIG

P.S. Do give my love to your wife and children. I trust that Gerhard is practicing night and day; please remind him that Prospero hovers over him unseen.

Uncle, you are mistaken if you think that my tune has changed; I'm every bit as eager now as I was three weeks ago to join the regiment. The obstacle, as you yourself just pointed out to Breuning, is the scar.

I don't know what "signs" you are speaking of.—With the exception of harvest day, I am utterly bored here. In fact I was about to suggest that we have a little party this evening.

To celebrate the completion of the new quartet. We should open a bottle of champagne and play some pieces together.

If Fat Stuff refuses, I'll pay for the wine out of my own pocket.

I stand corrected, out of *your pocket*.

You shouldn't blame *her* for that; she would hardly stint on wood if your brother didn't give the order.

I'm not trying to protect her. Yet considering how cheap wood is, I can't imagine what your brother has in mind. Why, a cord lasts an eternity.

Have I your permission to request the champagne?

And if they balk, may I say you'll pay for it yourself?

Well and good; and to warm up the fortress I'll bring Lannoy's Marches downstairs for us to play four hands.

———

Master Brother, Michael know from smile quartet finish.

After loud piano when everyone at table Mistress ask why Son not let Mistress play too.

Not with Son—why Master Brother not play with Mistress. Michael not understand how two play one piano.

Cook and Michael in dining room, not see only hear.

Four hand, Michael understand.

Son say piece too hard for Mistress. Mistress say Master Brother deaf so no matter.

She say piece hard for Master Brother too, make many mistake.

She say Master Brother play too loud.

She say Master Brother play too soft.

She say—but Michael not tell.

She say Master Brother play like bear.

Please Master Brother, Mistress hear shouting.

Son not say anything of four hand, only of quartet and who copy.

Now quartet finish Master Brother sleep late tomorrow?

Another quartet?

Then Michael bring hot water usual time.

———

Brother, I have combed the countryside but to no avail.

Money aside, there is simply not a copyist in all of Krems.

Would you consider permitting our nephew

It was just a thought.

In that case you have no choice but to undertake the job yourself.

———

Brother, the damned vulture postponed my taxes for a couple of days, yet not without exacting a hefty bribe—or *interest*, as he styles it. He'll look the other way until the 3rd. Hence the copying must be finished by the 30th—Will you be ready?

"Perhaps" is not good enough. Indeed I can't possibly go into town, deliver the score to the bookdealer and be back by the 3rd unless I leave at dawn on the 31st.

Mismanagement has nothing to do with it—I wouldn't be in this scrape if I hadn't had two extra mouths to feed.

Now let us pray that the dealer has received the 80 ducats as promised.

———

Uncle, the note to the bookdealer need not be lengthy.

GNEIXENDORF, OCTOBER 30, 1826

Sir!

I am sending you by my brother my latest violin quartet composed for Mr. Schlesinger; and I request you to hand to the former the fee of 80 ducats deposited with you for this purpose; and I herewith acknowledge receipt of said amount.

With kindest regards
your most devoted
LUDWIG VAN BEETHOVEN

Uncle, we might just as well attend to the other one now.

GNEIXENDORF, OCTOBER 30, 1826

My dear Schlesinger,

Just see what an unfortunate fellow I am. First of all, it has been difficult to compose this because I was thinking of a much greater work. I composed it solely because I had promised it to you and needed the money. That it was difficult for me to do so you can gather from the "It must be." But a further source of irritation was that in order to have it quite accurate and easy to engrave I wanted to send it to you in parts; and in all Krems I could not find a copyist. So I had to copy it myself. Well, that was a gruelling piece of work, I can assure you! Ugh, it is finished! Amen!

In great haste, your most devoted
BEETHOVEN

Uncle, I most certainly take what you say to heart; indeed I went again to Krems this morning, but the pharmacist still lacked one of the ingredients. Hence he could not compound the salve.

In my opinion the stuff is useless anyway since there is no sign of improvement.

Six weeks ago—I started applying it the day the bandages were removed, yet the scar is as noticeable now as it was then.

I've been without it for only three days.

What object could I possibly have in saying I apply the salve if, in fact, I don't?

Believe me, I'm bored to death here and cannot wait to depart.

Of course I'll continue using it, if you wish.

In that case before your brother leaves for town tomorrow, ask him to bring me back a fresh supply.

———

Brother, I'll thank you not to overburden me with errands since there is barely time to journey to town and back—Keep in mind that Wednesday is All Saints' Day. I'll certainly fetch the 80 ducats for you, and go to the banking house of Eskeles, and get hold of the salve for Karl. I'll also do my best to hunt up Holz and Schuppan-zigh—But beyond that I'll make no promises.

For my part I beg you *not to quarrel* with my wife. If she irks you, try to overlook it—or try at least to hold your fire until I return on Friday. Do keep in mind that she wishes only to please you.

Nevertheless she is at bottom perfectly harmless.

Spare me your puns—Have I your assurance that you'll keep the peace?

Even so, I'd appreciate your trying. Adieu.

———

Brother-in-law, you have misconstrued my laughter. I was prompted not by anything you did or said but by the tempo of the ending which left me breathless. I could hardly keep up with your nephew.

He plays the marches very well.

I'm not suggesting that he plays them better than you do.

Seeing that I've never heard a bear play, I have no opinion.

That's a brazen lie! I really can't imagine who fabricated such a lie.

Then your brother was joking. What I said, to be exact, is that whether you play four hands or solo, you always play like a Master. In fact I would be honored if you deigned now to play with me.

In that case perhaps you'll oblige me tomorrow. Do have a restful night.

———

Uncle, I brought down the Haydn only because some of the pieces are easier than the ones we played last night, and Fat Stuff was still hoping to play four hands.

Not with me, she was hoping to play *with you*.

You! you! you! I accompanied her only because you refused.

Needless to say, there is not room at the keyboard to place the chairs more widely.

Presumably she removed her stole to free her arms.

I didn't note the talcum powder.

Nor the perfume.

Naturally her shoulder touched mine, how could it be otherwise?
She is a very big woman. Why, even when you and I play four hands

You are utterly mistaken if you think that she "pressed herself"
against me.

I don't know what you are aiming at or, rather, I *do* know and find
the notion ludicrous.

But I told you at the time that I had no such interest, none whatever
in Niemetz's mother. My only reason for staying there overnight was
that I lacked funds to stay at an inn—Besides, she had lent me a
book that I

Roman Elegies

You are not "on the scent" of anything. The line that I cited on harvest day has no bearing

"Darling, why didn't you come to meet me in the vineyard today?"

God is my witness, I have no such interest in Fat Stuff.

If you don't believe me, then let us drop the subject.

May I be excused?

To go to my room, naturally.

Good night, Uncle.

———

Master Brother, Michael understand. Watch Son in night like soldier from passage outside dressing room.

Behind door? How watch Son if door shut?

Open crack, Michael understand. When Son leave room tell Master Brother where Son go.

Favor for Michael please before watch.

Go home come back 10 minutes.

Tonight not like harvest night. If not home father beat.

Not with cane. Father not have cane. Schoolmaster have cane.

Father of Master Brother beat with cane?

Father of Michael beat with horse strap.

Strap not bad as cane.

Schoolmaster once break boy rib.

Rib of Master Brother break?

Stop talk of beating?

Thank you favor Master Brother. Michael run both way.

————

Brother-in-law, good morning. I trust that last night's little storm has blown

Since Michael didn't appear for work I assumed he was ill; thus I took it upon myself to serve the hot water.

Only after I came upstairs did I find the no-good asleep on the floor.

And what, if I may ask, was the object of his vigil?

I'm sorry to hear that. Are your bowels poor again?

I sent him back downstairs where he belongs. You ought to take hot chocolate with breakfast.

Hot chocolate would be better than tea, especially if you've been belching.

As you wish. Breakfast will be served at the usual hour.

———

Brother-in-law, do try to calm yourself—I'll explain everything if only

I can't explain if you

Uncle, it's useless to make such a commotion without knowing what

But Michael isn't here.

He has been discharged.

Please, you'll have an apoplexy if you don't stop shouting.

That is what she is trying to report, if you would only let her.

Brother-in-law, since your health had improved so markedly, nay, miraculously by breakfast time I resolved to serve you a proper dinner. To that end I gave Michael 5 gulden and sent him off to Krems to fetch a salmon and a bottle of your favorite wine. At 10:30 I began to consider what sort of misfortune might have befallen the boy. By 11 I had to consider what to substitute for the salmon. I hit upon croquettes, inasmuch as they

In brief, when the no-good finally showed up at 11:30 he was empty-handed. I asked him where the provisions were, but he could only hem and haw. I then asked if they had been stolen; again he couldn't find his tongue, not even to fabricate a lie. Thereupon I asked to have the money back. Still, he neither spoke *nor* returned the money. Only when I took him by the ear and demanded an explanation did he stammer "lost." Thus I threw the scoundrel out! And when your brother returns tomorrow you may be sure that I'll have the little thief hauled before the Magistrate!

Are the coins which you have flung at me meant to make good my loss?

Very well, if you insist I'll bring him back. However, there is still the matter of the theft.

Unlike you I'm not the least convinced that Michael

Then let us wait until your brother

In that case I'll excuse myself.

Uncle, I beg of you not to be so agitated.

But she agreed to bring him back.

Indeed she left the table for that very reason: to send for him.

I have no idea where Slut went; she merely asked to be excused. Doubtless your outburst unstrung her.

Well and good, but you can't bar them from your brother's table.

I don't follow you.

All of them? Surely it would be better, if only for propriety's sake, to take one meal a day in the dining room.

Do please reconsider.

Then let us hope your absence doesn't worsen matters.

———

Brother, I'm sorry to find you in poor health.

Granted these attacks are nothing new, yet there is no question of their injuriousness—they can easily lead to an inflamation of the bowels. When did it start?

Of course I've brought the money—we reached town well before offices closed for the holiday.

I'll thank you not to cry cheat so quickly—I've simply deducted 40 gulden for this month's room and board.

Let's not rehearse our finances yet again—Holz sends you his fondest embraces; he is still very much in the ecstasy of love—Naturally! the man is but two months wed. He and Linke, who by the way also sends greetings, are most eager to have the new finale. I told them that if all goes well it should be ready in three or four weeks.

Excellent, the sooner the better.

Unfortunately I didn't find time for Karl's salve. However, since it is not particularly effective—Why do you keep spitting into your handkerchief?

Thank Heaven there is none, but do stop spitting so harshly or you are apt to produce some.

Of course I've not forgotten that you spat blood last year, nor have I forgotten that our mother and brother died of consumption, yet it doesn't follow a priori that you'll share their fate—Have you any appetite?

What has my wife been serving you?

Eggs and cheese can do you no harm but the soup should be rice, only rice—I'll advise her. And to drink?

Good God! wine is out of the question.

Diluted or not makes no difference; wine in any form is strictly forbidden—I'll order a tonic.

I don't follow you.

But if Michael didn't bring the wine from Krems and you didn't drink it, I fail to see how my wife

Come now, you have no reason to suspect her—When our brother died you were certain that Johanna had poisoned him, yet the autopsy disproved your suspicion.

At least I understand now why you refuse to take your meals with her.

Believe me, Brother, my wife entertains no such wicked schemes.

Would it set your mind at ease if at meals she were to taste the wine before you do?

If not—Even so I ask you to come back to the table.

Tant pis!

———

Uncle, a reply has come from Breuning.

VIENNA, NOVEMBER 6, 1826

My dear Ludwig,

Today I took the opportunity to have a word with the Lieutenant Field-Marshal and am pleased to report that he is no less inclined than he was in September to give your nephew a cadetship. At the same time he questioned me, quite understandably, about the length of the convalescence. As you will doubtless recall, I told him in September that Karl was recovering from a hernia operation; hence today I compounded the case by fabricating a "slight infection." Even so, let us not arouse his suspicions by prolonging the dissimulation. Surely a clever hand will find a way to dress the hair in a manner that conceals the scar. Besides, now that the last quartet is finished and winter is coming on apace, I urge you to return forthwith. If Karl is to have a career and you are to have your health, you must not procrastinate.

Gerhard has been practicing no less than an hour a day and sometimes more; in his not dispassionate opinion, with which I more or less concur, his fingering is much improved. As for his interpretation, he awaits your return with fluctuating fear and impatience.

I earnestly hope to see you soon. Meanwhile my family joins me in sending our warmest embraces.

With love, your most devoted
STEPHAN

Uncle, with due respect to Breuning there is not a hairdresser in all of Austria clever enough to conceal the scar.

Then your brother should have made more of an effort to obtain the salve.

Nevertheless I can't be introduced to the Field-Marshal with the scar in its present state—Oh what I wouldn't give for hair like yours.

Certainly not! Your brother's hair is no thicker than mine; besides, everybody knows he dyes it.

In truth we have no choice but to stay a while longer; let's stay at least until the new finale is finished.

———

GNEIXENDORF, NOVEMBER 11, 1826

Dear Tobias,

Since you did not reply to my first letter, I did not wish to trouble you any further. So I sent my brother off to Vienna with my latest quartet.

Now I have one more request to make. A small parcel for Matthias Artaria is being sent to your address. As soon as it arrives, please let him know that the parcel is with you. But you must give it to him only against a payment of 15 gold ducats. Just say that you

Uncle, it's clear that you are in pain.

Surely the letter can wait until your brother brings the liniment. In the meantime I'll make up the parcel with the new finale. By the way, you should ask Uncle Johann to be on the lookout for someone to carry it into town.

Since he got back but a week ago I doubt that he'll be willing to return so soon. What is more, if you do speak of it be prepared for a lengthy exposition on the wear and tear to the wheels, the splashboard, the spring, etc.

Still, the manuscript cannot be entrusted to just anyone. In all likelihood your brother will know of—But here he is.

Brother, the basin which Michael holds contains the volatile liniment.

A perfectly mild lotion of ammonia water and sesame oil. Once the cloth is applied to your belly the ammonia will evaporate—hence the designation volatile—therewith easing the pain.

Come now, disrobe.

Why do you hesitate?

Our nephew and Michael hardly constitute an audience—In any case they must learn for themselves how to apply the compress.

Never fear—soups are served piping hot, the lotion is lukewarm.

There now, is that not better?

I don't follow you.

I don't assume anything of the sort—Why would the simple act of doctoring your belly suggest such an ambition?

Rest assured that I have no designs on your title—Ever since our mother's death you have been head of the family and head you shall remain.

Instead of defaming me you might just thank me for my trouble.

I sent him from the room because Michael is a servant and there is work to be done.

Our nephew says that you've finished the new finale and are looking for someone to deliver it to Haslinger for you.

Certainly not—Why, have you any idea how much it costs me every time I run the carriage between Gneixendorf

I'll do my best to find you someone trustworthy—Better still, you should consider delivering it yourself.

May I read his letter?

Not only do I agree with Breuning but I urge you to heed his advice.

For your sake not mine, but especially for Karl's sake.

What object could I have but for him to get on with his career?

Believe me, I have no other object.

Why don't you believe me?

Now it's my turn to query you—Why did you send our nephew from the room?

Your assumption is utterly false, not to say foolish—You have sunk as low as Beaumarchais if you imagine

On no occasion—never have I found them seated together at the piano, nor have I noted any whispering or exchanging of glances en passant or stroking with the fingertips or any other show of interest on either side—*Never!*

You are utterly wrong if you think it has anything to do with my wife—I'm urging you to leave only because I can't afford to have you stay.

Of course I haven't forgotten the 40 gulden—do you take me for a common thief! On the other hand the cost of essentials increases with the bad weather. Why, candles, fuel, boot polish—indeed *everything* costs more in winter. Besides, your ill health brings all sorts of unexpected expenses.

Medicines for one, chocolate for another—At the same time your soiled linen requires the use of additional soap and bleach, and beyond that there is Seltzer-water and

True enough, but let me tell you this—our nephew makes up twofold for the wine you are not drinking.

He takes one glass more with every meal—at the least, sometimes two! Worse still, hardly a day now passes without a game of billiards.

I didn't say that he is gambling, nor did I mean to imply it—Yet must it come to that before you heed my advice and take an early departure?

Well and good, but you do so at your own risk.

———

Master Brother, Mistress not see wine—glass under jacket.

Master Brother not add water?

Michael fetch.

Yes Son drink more wine.

1 more dinner.

2 more supper.

Son same chair—side of Daughter.

Mistress same chair.

Master Brother chair empty.

Michael understand, fetch Son.

———

Uncle, you sent for me?

From time to time perhaps.

A glass or two.

Your brother exaggerates, I never take more than three.

Indeed I do play occasionally. Is billiards now forbidden?

So long as we are confined here, I need some sort of recreation. What would your brother have me do?

Were it not for the scar, I too would urge you to heed their advice. But as you see, there is no improvement to speak of.

Although I'm not opposed to leaving, I would in truth prefer to stay.

If only because the longer we stay, the longer we may stay together.

What is the matter, why do you turn away?

I'm sorry, I didn't mean to sadden your heart.

But you have no grounds to doubt my sincerity.

Fat Stuff be damned, it's you I wish to be with.

On my honor.

Don't fret about your brother; somehow he'll reconcile himself to our staying a while longer.

———

Brother, I realize that you've doctored yourself already, but do allow me to examine your belly.

Such trickery—you fool no one but yourself!

It's obvious that Michael brings you wine in secret.

Because the swelling does not go down—if anything it appears worse. Perhaps that accounts for your not having taken your walk this morning—I saw no sign of you in the fields.

Your feet too—May I see them?

Kindly remove your socks.

Thus far they are only moderately swollen, thank goodness.

No, the two are not related—the swelling of the belly is caused by inflammation, that of the feet by an accumulation of fluid—All the more reason then to hurry back to town—you cannot wait until they are dropsical and need to be drained.

Indeed I didn't forget—my friend Sterz would be more than pleased, nay, honored to deliver the new finale to Haslinger. Unfortunately he doesn't plan to travel to Vienna for another week, not until the 23rd.

Why do you insist upon delaying?

For the hundredth time—*My wife entertains no such fancy for our nephew.*

In that case you'll have to wait until doomsday!

Because I'll never see for myself something that is but a figment of your imagination.

If in fact you believe what you say, you would do well to rescue him.

By leaving here at once!

I've known some pigheaded men, Brother, but you surely take the cake.

Brother, your belly appears somewhat better this morning. I'll wager that if you continue to respect the regimen, we'll soon see further improvement—Well now, where is the new finale?

Although it's only the 21st today, I won't be going to Krems again before Sterz leaves on Thursday. Is the parcel not ready?

Don't be the least concerned, I'll give him strict instructions on how to get to Haslinger's shop—Am I to mention the 15 ducats?

In that case I'll say nothing—Now for more pressing matters, namely, our nephew.

Karl must not stay in Gneixendorf another week, not beyond this Sunday—He must not make use of his scar to dawdle here—If, as Breuning says, the boy is to have a career, he must leave for Iglau at once—And you Ludwig, you must not be so indecisive; you must lay down the law to him—Fix a date for your departure and then stick by it! You simply must not permit

Instead of finding the *musts* so distasteful, you would do better to chew the meat.

Why do you smile? Will you not take seriously

I don't follow you—*what* in fact have you been waiting for?

Indeed I haven't! Nor will I ever catch them in flagrante delicto— Don't be such an ass!

Of course I'm certain, as certain of their innocence

Their guilt exists solely in your imagination.

Ah! so now it's my turn to hear your catalogue of *musts*.

Absolutely not!

Under no circumstances will I change my testament.

Not only won't I cut off my wife, I'll thank you

Insist until hell freezes over—I'll not comply.

If our nephew is to salvage his young life, you won't make your departure dependent upon the changing of my will—In fact if you wish to avert disaster, you'll

I have it on good authority that he is gambling again.

My steward—the man saw Karl wagering with some laborers.

At a low-class tavern in Krems—Before we know it there will be a repetition of last summer's tragedy.

Raise your arms overhead

Don't try to speak—just drink the water

I didn't mean to cause you such distress—Still, you must nip it in the bud, put an end once for all to the slothful life he is leading here.

Why would you have me fetch Michael—it's Karl whom

Very well, if I see the lad I'll send him up to you.

———

Master Brother, wish Michael clean room now?

Son leave house after breakfast.

Clean Son room now?

Not clean?

Search instead, I understand. Search where?

Search wardrobe and chest and night stand and

Everywhere, I understand.

Wait because Master Brother not say what Michael search *for*.

Not afraid—surprise.

Go search at once.

———

Uncle, when I returned for my muffler I found your favorite here ransacking my room—Thus Fat Stuff was right after all, he is indeed a thief.

In that case perhaps you'll tell me what he was searching for?

Kindly send Michael out so that we may speak freely.

What made you fear that I had a pistol?

On whose good authority?

I fail to see the connection between wagering at billiards and purchasing a pistol.

What happened in July was brought on by your constant and, I may say, unjust reproaches, not to mention your everlasting suspicions about money, whereas now we have no such quarrels. Besides, it's not for the money that I wager but simply to enliven the game.

Three or four times in all; on no occasion did I wager more than 30 kreuzer.

On my honor.

With the pocket money which I saved.

But I haven't sought additional funds, nor have I any need of them. What are you insinuating?

But I've not had to borrow a penny; I had the good fortune to win right off.

A strict accounting of what?

Not again! With all due respect I am now twenty-one years

I realize that I won't reach my majority until I am twenty-four, nevertheless

I would remind you that our worst quarrels last year came from your insistence that I keep a strict accounting of all receipts and expenditures. I beg you not to re-impose

I'm concealing nothing.

It's not a question of the money but of

Nobody at my age is made to

If I'm old enough to join

Never—under no circumstances will I render an accounting.

In that case you had better send for Holz!

To spy on me!

———

No, Brother-in-law, he said nothing before leaving the house.

No, in truth I've never heard him say a word against you. Indeed your nephew loves you to the point of veneration.

What object could I have in dissimulating? Rest assured that what I say is true.

In the direction of Krems.

I very much doubt that he plans to play billiards at this hour. Still, it's obvious that he is bored here and should join his regiment as soon as possible.

And now with regard to domestic maters, your servant tells me that your stomach is improved. Will you take the entree with dinner?

Hare in cream sauce.

Then soup and eggs it will be.

———

Master Brother, Son return from Krems.

In salon with Master.

Mistress with Daughter.

Mistress bring Daughter dinner to room.

Daughter ill.

But this *your* tray, not for Daughter.

Not hare, cream soup and eggs, strictly 3 minute.

Michael not forget but Mistress say throw Michael out if Michael bring wine.

Please not scold Mistress.

If Master Brother not scold Mistress Mistress not scold Michael.

Thank you Master Brother.

———

Master Brother, Master say give letter with breakfast.

My dear Brother,

I cannot possibly remain silent concerning Karl's future. He is growing slothful here and habituated to this way of life; the longer he goes on in this fashion, the more unfortunate it will be for him. When we set out for Gneixendorf, Breuning gave him a fortnight to recuperate, and now it is two months—You see from Breuning's letter that it is his express wish for Karl to *hurry* to his calling; the longer he is here the more difficult it will be for him to resume work, and we may be the ones to suffer the consequences.

It is an infinite pity that this talented young man so wastes his time; and on whom if not *the two of us* will the blame fall? For he is still too young to steer his own course; therefore it is your duty, if you do not wish to be reproached by yourself and others hereafter, to make him start his career at once. The moment he is not idle it will be easy to do a good deal for him; but at present nothing can be done.

I see from his actions that he would like to stay here, but if he were to do so it would spell ruin for his future; thus *he must depart.* The longer you hesitate the more dificult it will be for him to tear himself away; I therefore entreat you—make up your mind, don't permit him to talk you out of it. I think it ought to be by *next*

Monday. In no event can you wait for me, inasmuch as I cannot leave here without *money*, and it will be a long time before I collect enough to go to Vienna.

No, Master Brother, Master only say bring letter.

Son in dining room.

Now or after breakfast?

I fetch him.

———

All else aside, Uncle, your brother is mistaken; believe me, I have no wish to stay here.

I'm at a loss to explain his object; but rest assured that I'll leave without delay the moment the scar permits.

Clearly my future doesn't turn on whether it's a Monday or Tuesday. The whole thing smacks of the theater.

More pressing, however, than your brother's letter is the note to Haslinger which must accompany the new finale. Do dictate it now.

GNEIXENDORF, NOVEMBER 22

I am sending you herewith, though a little later than I intended, the parcel about which I have already informed you. Please deliver it to Matthias Artaria who will pay you 15 ducats for it. Should I be in a position to return your kindness, I shall not fail to do so.

Your most devoted
BEETHOVEN

P.S. Please give the bearer a few lines stating that you have received the above-mentioned parcel.

Uncle, your brother is making his rounds now, but I'll be glad to take it to Sterz.

If I'm not to be trusted, then by all means have your brother take it to him.

Hardly a ruse—Need I contrive a ruse in order to go to Krems?

Surely there is no call for that. You have my word that I will not gamble. Isn't that sufficient? Must I ask your permission henceforth to go to Krems?

And must I also ask your permission to walk in the fields?

If I appear insolent, perhaps your stringent rules are to blame—I'm simply too old to be supervised in this fashion.

There you are wrong; I would leave here this minute were the scar less conspicuous.

Certainly not, there is no one, nothing—nothing whatever holds me here. I can't imagine what your brother had in mind.

I just now said that I don't know. If you do, fine! But then why ask me?

Why do you raise your voice? I can hear you perfectly well without

I'm unaware of having rolled my eyes. If indeed I did, I meant no disrespect; it's only because we've been over the question of your sister-in-law a dozen times.

For the simple reason that I've nothing to confess.

I've sworn on my honor that I take no interest in her—What more would you have me say?

Naturally I heard you, doubtless you were heard in Krems.

On the contrary my silence signifies disdain—it's beneath me to refute such accusations.

Why, when you already have my word?

Well and good, I give you my word that I am not fornicating with Fat Stuff. There! Are you now satisfied?

I am not lying!

Then let us drop the subject.

Kindly refrain from saying that.

It's pointless to make a scene.

You have only to drop the subject in order to

Please, I beg of you to drop

But I *have* told you the truth!

I have—I have!!!

I cannot answer in this state.

When I've stopped.

I'm ashamed of myself for weeping. After what happened in July I wouldn't have thought it possible for you ever to bring me to tears again. In fact, it was for just that reason, to forestall such a tirade, that I was silent earlier. Indeed I fail to see what is to be gained by raking up past misdeeds, I mean *alleged* misdeeds or by reviving old reproaches. If, as you assert, I lied to you, let alone your secretaries and my schoolmasters, about visiting my mother—or even if I lied about stealing the housekeeper's money for chocolates—For God's sake, that was years ago! Because I lied to you when I was twelve, doesn't mean I'm lying now.

Please don't begin again.

You may accuse me of anything you like, I'll simply accept what you say in silence, as is my duty.

Did you see me speak? Hardly. No matter what you say about Niemetz and his mother or about your sister-in-law, I'll not refute it—Thus I ask you to stop.

I'll hear nothing about my mother!

If you don't stop

I beg you once for all not to torment me as you are doing now or you may regret it.

Put whatever construction on it you like.

Why do you make such a scene?

I've had enough!

For a walk.

But I've not been outside today.

I need a breath of air.

Not even to the garden?

In that case I'll go to my room.

Is there no place you'll let me go!

Because I need to be by myself.

But I must be!

To my room

I only wish to go to my room!

Will you not let me go to my room?

I will not endure this!

———

Yes, Brother-in-law, he ran from the house in tears.

Five minutes ago.

I did my best but couldn't stop him.

He had no pistol, of that I am certain.

In the direction of the fields.

Do reconsider, your feet are too swollen to go after him.

Fear not, no harm will come to him.

Of course you'll see him again and, I dare say, in time for dinner. Do take heart.

Because it's nothing but a passing squall; he'll return as soon as he regains his composure.

It would seem that he has some of your hot blood—one might even say that it runs in the Beethoven family.

For heaven's sake don't take offense, I was only joking.

Look!

No, beyond the oxcart—Isn't that your nephew?

So, as you see, I was right.

He appears to be coming back. Before I return to my duties, let me urge you to heed your brother's advice.

Your nephew should leave here without delay.

Why do you look surprised?

Naturally I agree with my husband.

You have no reason to doubt me. In fact I feel more strongly than my husband does that your nephew should leave here at once. Can't you see the necessity?

But the scar is hardly noticeable. Besides if you stay, there will doubtless be further squalls; and that can't help but harm your health.

Thank Heaven! My husband will be greatly pleased.

Here now is your nephew—I'll excuse myself.

Uncle, surely my absence was too brief to cite the prodigal son.

In any case I've returned.

Whenever you decide to leave, rest assured that I'll abide by your decision.

Am I now permitted to go to my room?

Thank you for your clemency.

———

Master Brother, Michael not understand.

Master Brother wish Michael also go?

To Vienna!

All life since boy Michael—cannot find word.

No, always wish Vienna, dream Vienna.

Father surely forbid.

Michael ask tonight, tell tomorrow.

Coachman in stable.

Name Josef. Michael fetch?

Stable too far, Michael fetch.

Master Brother feet bad, Michael fetch.

After breakfast Michael bring Master Brother see Josef.

———

Master Brother, Josef say need one day ahead for carriage.

Master Brother wish carriage Monday, Michael understand.

Josef say carriage order Monday.

Carriage *already* order Monday.

Josef say Master order carriage.

Josef laugh because Master Brother say horse blanket better than blanket on bed.

Josef thank for coin.

Master Brother wish speak with Master, Michael understand.

———

Brother, you misconstrue—I have no such scheme in mind. My own wishes aside, I could hardly force you to leave against your will—Indeed the carriage is ordered not for you but for my wife who has business in town with her brother.

Bravissimo! I can't tell you how much that pleases me—the more, since it signifies your willingness to travel with my wife.

You are forgetting that there were three of us when we came here.

In that case I'll send my wife by coach and you and Karl may have the carriage.

I simply can't afford to send it back and forth twice—Come now, reconsider.

But since you needn't speak to my wife along the way and needn't take your meals with her, and since, moreover, our nephew's future hinges on his leaving Monday, I beg you to swallow your distaste and travel with the woman.

Believe me, it's imperative!

Oh, thank you, Brother—I embrace you.

———

Uncle, if you wish to leave this Monday, fine.

If not, fine again; Wednesday will serve equally well.

Why do your eyes bore into me so?

Monday or Friday, it's all the same to me.

Indeed I had no idea that Fat Stuff was going to Vienna this Monday. In that case let us leave the following week.

But if you've already made up your mind to leave on Monday, it's useless to dwell on the subject.

Rest assured that I'll be ready first thing Monday morning.

———

Master Brother, Michael not see Vienna.

Father forbid.

Michael sorry too, also sorry Master Brother leave Monday.

Not leave Monday?

Pack bag but not leave? Michael not understand.

Never see play in Krems.

Not truly pack bag?

Truly pack bag but not truly leave.

Pretend?

Only pretend Master Brother leave, Michael understand.

Not tell Son.

Not tell Mistress.

Michael not tell no one.

———

Brother, it's much too cold to stand out here—do get into the carriage.

It's Amalie—my wife is taking the girl with her.

It was decided only last night.

There is no difference between three and four—Now do get in.

Make haste! If Josef is to reach St. Polten by nightfall, he must

Say no more—I'll have the women climb out—they can travel by coach.

Hold on! Don't have Karl climb out—My wife's business can wait, Karl's cannot.

I told him to get back in.

I implore you not to undo the entire plan.

Then have Karl get back in.

For God's sake, *tell him to get in!*

So be it—It's on your own head!

I ordered Josef to set out with the women as soon as Michael takes down your bags.

Tant pis! You'll just have to wait now until I'm good and ready.

———

Uncle, perhaps it would be better to let your brother cool down for a while; there will be ample time this evening to raise the subject.

It's *you* who are cold; he is piping hot.

In that case shall I tell him he'll find you in the sitting room?

If your feet are frozen, don't mount the stairs. I'll say that you are in the salon.

———

Brother, the fact that you meddled with our brother's will gives you no license to meddle with mine. Surely I made myself clear on this last week—Let's say no more about it.

That is none of your affair—Still, you are wrong to assume that Therese is my sole beneficiary—she has her share and will get no more.

When our brother signed that codicil appointing you Karl's guardian he was on his deathbed, whereas I am in the best of health, thank God! Besides, it was executed at your insistence and in return for helping our brother during his illness—Well, fortunately I have no need of your financial help—Indeed the opposite has been the case for twenty years.

Since the first loan I made you was in 1807—Very well, it's nineteen years—Don't let's quibble.

Seeing that I didn't purchase the apothecary shop in Linz until 1808, Therese was not even in the picture.

Frankly I don't see what bearing any of this has on my wife.

Don't imagine that by defaming Therese you'll persuade me to make my estate over to Karl—certainly not! On that I am adamant.

If you insist on discussing the matter, be so good as to send our nephew out of the room.

As soon as you send him out, I'll tell you.

His presence hinders my speaking freely.

Suit yourself—It's not with my wife that the young man has been debauching himself but with her daughter.

My wife discovered them a week ago.

In the linen press.

Suffice it to say that they were en déshabillé.

If you don't believe me, you have only to question Karl.

No, Uncle, I cannot deny it.

It happened in drunkenness.

Of course I see how incensed you are.

I have nothing more to say.

Because nothing but silence can follow such a tirade.

On the contrary I remember perfectly what you said about the pestilence of whores.

But I heeded your advice.

Between you and me, I never entered there; in fact I never ventured anywhere near the "swampy place."

Believe me, Uncle, we did not make the beast with two backs.

So, Brother, you see now why the girl was sent packing, to say nothing of why I won't cut off my wife.

Be reasonable—my wife is utterly blameless.

Rubbish! she initiated no such thing.

You disgrace us both with this kind of talk.

After being told that my wife is the mother of her daughter's lust and that both are whores, I'm asked once more to alter my will—Go to the devil!

Karl will have more than enough with your bank shares.

Away with that shit—he'll get nothing from me.

Being head of the family doesn't make you head of this estate. It's *mine*—my property, acquired by the sweat of my brow and the ingenuity of my business dealings. So I'll thank you not to dictate my heirs to me.

I grant you that he is our flesh and blood—on the other hand she is my wife.

Be careful, Ludwig—*scum* is what you called her fourteen years ago when she was still my housekeeper.

Well and good, housekeeper-cum-paramour—which, needless to say, is what prompted you to besiege us in Linz—By God! but you were treacherous.

Not treacherous to disgrace the girl publicly! Why, you stopped at nothing to make me break with her—indeed you brought me to the brink of desperation! And when I came to your room to give you a piece of my mind, you flew into a rage and took me by the throat— Was that not treachery! Well, no matter—in return you received a thrashing the likes of which you'll never forget!

Frankly you have no one but yourself to thank, since it was you who provoked, nay, drove me—*you drove me to marry her.*

If you hadn't gone to the Bishop and railed against the girl—worse still, if you hadn't obtained a police order banishing her from Linz— Who knows, perhaps I would never have married Therese; I did so only to revenge myself on you.

I warn you, Ludwig

Don't persist in saying

On the contrary it's *you* who are lacking in manhood!

Capon!

Worm!

I'll thrash you again!

Enough, I say!!!

Uncle, I had no choice but to intervene.

To prevent bloodshed.

Please sit down.

It does no good to keep calling him Cain.

What he just said is immaterial.

I beg of you to sit down.

Brother, now that you've left the field I'll tell you what I said. For thirty years I've had to stomach your calling me Cain, in spite of the fact—which everyone in Christendom but you knows—that Cain was the *older* brother. Thus I merely remarked that for once you happened to be right—for surely I would have finished you off, had you not cried out for mercy.

Come now, don't let's start again.

You did indeed cry out.

"Don't hit me!" were your words.

If you don't believe me, ask our nephew.

Uncle, unfortunately I failed to hear what was said.

Brother, clearly our nephew is dissimulating, but let it pass—As for my will, it stands—I'll not alter a word.

That's enough! If I were you and found myself in such miserable health, I would depart posthaste and not look back until I reached Vienna.

Well and good, but there is no postchaise from here.

If you hadn't undone the plan, you would be halfway there by now.

You'll have to take the coach from St. Polten.

Do as you please—I must make my rounds.

———

Uncle, your brother spoke the truth: one must travel by stagecoach from St. Polten.

Everything you say about the tortures of the rack, your swollen feet and belly, the riffraff and pigsty is true; yet there is no other possibility, one must travel by coach.

Most likely your brother's carriage will return Thursday.

I doubt that he'll agree to send it back so soon.

Under those circumstances he might, providing that the sum is large enough.

Since you refuse to travel by coach, his carriage is the only alternative.

Do try your best to reach an accommodation.

———

Brother, I expect the carriage Thursday afternoon.

You've forgotten that Friday is December 1st—taxes! Doubtless that hellhound is already sharpening his claws for me.

I can't possibly send it back that soon—not in fact for many weeks.

Because I can't afford it.

Well, that's a different story—What sum have you in mind?

You must be jesting.

Is that your best offer?

Then let us drop the subject.

I said let it be.

Enough of your filthy aspersions!

Not if you offered me 500!

I kiss my hand to you!

You'll simply have to travel by coach as others do.

————

But, Uncle, we are going around in circles—there is no other possibility.

Be reasonable, you cannot travel by farm wagon.

I don't doubt that there are wagons for hire, yet it's out of the question; one cannot travel by open wagon in December.

Whether or not it's rigged with canvas, the sides will still be open.

Before you send for Michael, please let me speak to your brother.

Let me try at least to persuade him.

————

Money aside, Uncle; firstly, your brother dwelled on the wear and tear to the carriage and horses; secondly, he spoke of Breuning and the Field-Marshal, thirdly

In short he flatly refused and entreated you to take the coach.

I beg of you to listen to reason.

Unfortunately you are spiting no one but yourself.

The wagon is secondary; the trick will be to find a farmer ready to leave at once.

Alas, your resolve is unmistakable; I'll tell Michael to make inquiries.

———

Master Brother, farmer say ready Friday.

Cannot leave Gneixendorf Friday arrive Vienna Friday, must stop for night.

Not St. Polten, farmer say Mitterndorf better.

What time you wish farmer fetch?

Still too dark, not see road so early.

Crack of dawn, Michael understand.

———

Brother, even if you are wedded to the wagon, at least travel to St. Polten by postchaise. From there you can easily

Mitterndorf—why on earth would the man go by way of Mitterndorf?

Never mind shorter—the road is simply wretched.

Why will you never heed my advice!

In that case I'll say no more.

———

Master Brother, Michael understand. Tomorrow hot water with breakfast, take bag down, load bag on wagon, come back, help Son help Master Brother down.

Take blanket please.

Coat for September not December, wear blanket over coat please.

Blanket from bed not horse blanket.

Farmer say wagon reach Vienna Saturday.

Late afternoon.

Michael not smile because not see Palace or St Stephen church or Prater park, and not hear new quartet.

But Master Brother make quartet, not need hear.

God forgive—Michael stupid!

Please forgive—Michael stupid ass!

Master Brother very kind but not true. Father forbid Vienna not because Michael smart, father need Michael help.

If Michael disobey and go with Master Brother, father beat.

Michael never say not hit me.

Father of Master Brother say not hit me? Master Brother hit father!

Master Brother honor father, son always honor father.

Son not always honor Master Brother?

Michael not understand fil—cannot write.

Filial piety, Michael, is duty to one's father.

Son not show duty?

Not good Michael show more duty than Son?

Michael too wish to be Master Brother son.

Michael leave room because of tears.

Not in pocket?

Maybe sleeve.

Why reward? Michael not find handkerchief, Master Brother find.

Thank you Master Brother.

Michael too never forget Master Brother.

Take tray now?

Good night Master Brother, thank you so much for gold ducat.

———

Brother, I beseech you to reconsider.

Not another word about the carriage—it's *you* who must come to your senses.

Pigheaded! Pigheaded! Pigheaded!

My wife has come to bid you adieu.

Can you not be civil even in parting!

I merely told our nephew and Michael to help you downstairs. However, first you must pay me for that blanket.

Do calm yourself!

Evidently our nephew agrees with you.

My apologies—the two blankets are all but indistinguishable. Doubtless you'll need it in your humble conveyance.

Blankets aside, I hope you have a comfortable, I mean swift journey—*utterly prestissimo!*

Farewell, Brother.

4

THE GRAND piano, Uncle. You are in your own apartment, your own bed in Schwarzpanier House.

It's Sunday morning, December 3rd; we arrived here last night.

Don't try to move, the pain is worse when you lie on your back. I'll hold the cup for you.

Only hot water, it relieves the cough.

You've been in this misery since Friday night.

I'll tell you everything as soon as we send for a doctor.

That is what you said last night, yet neither the fever nor the pain has subsided. Do let me send for a doctor.

But earlier you spat blood—you can't be left to languish.

In my opinion Dr. Braunhofer would be the best of the three.

Then let us send for him at once.

It needn't be in your own hand; I'll take it down.

My honored friend,

I am in severe pain and hope that I may count on you once more for help. I earnestly beg you to come to me at your earliest convenience, if possible even as early as this morning. A thousand thanks in advance for your unfailing care.

Your most devoted and grateful

BEETHOVEN

Uncle, in the time that I wasted finding a carriage the maid could have walked to Braunhofer's.

I told her to wait for an answer.

Sali said that you took a cup of tea while I was out. Did it soothe your throat?

The cough, as well as the other complaints, began on Friday night.

Even before we reached Mitterndorf you were chilled to the bone.

Now that the doctor is sent for I'll write out a brief account of what happened at The Golden Stag.

From the moment that we crossed the bridge at Mautern and traveled along the riverside road there was no shelter from the freezing wind, let alone the damp; moreover the sun failed to break through all day. At Traismauer you ate a steaming plate of soup, but to no avail since we had to travel another six hours before reaching The Golden Stag.—The Dying Stag would better describe an inn with a ruined front, broken floorboards and slanting tables; in short, with everything in such disrepair that one would not think of stopping there overnight. On the other hand you were shivering and utterly miserable. Thus when the proprietor said he could accommodate us, it seemed a stroke of fortune, the more so since the room was on the ground floor which spared you the stairs. Of course the scoundrel failed to mention that it was equipped with neither a stove nor shutters. In point of fact one could see one's breath indoors! Looking back, I suspect that the room is let solely in summer, save to dupes like us.

After supper I had no difficulty persuading you to get into the bed; you did so with alacrity. Whereupon I spread all three blankets over you and sat down at the table. About ten o'clock you started coughing violently and groaning with pain, but by and by the fit subsided, indeed you even dozed. It was not long, however, before the coughing resumed; worse still, you complained of a hellish thirst. Unfortunately the water in the room was ice-cold, hence I went to fetch another jug from the proprietor. When I knocked at his door there was no answer, so naturally I knocked again. Yet no matter how many times I knocked, he did not answer. Clearly the villain was feigning sleep, for even after I gave the door a swift kick he did not stir.

Upon returning to the room I found you at the table with a cup in one hand and the jug, already half-empty, in the other—notwithstanding the ice-cold water, you had got up to slake your thirst. As you were still coughing I begged you to get back into the bed, but you refused. Nor would you relinquish the jug. Indeed you clasped it to you defiantly and sat down at the table. There being but one chair in the room I covered you with the blankets from the bed and stretched myself on the crude mattress. In spite of the cold I, too, must have dozed for suddenly something woke me with a start. It was the jug which had slipped from your hands and broken. When I stooped to gather up the pieces there was scarcely a drop of water on the floor; you had, alas, quaffed it all. An instant later the proprietor's wife was at the door demanding to know what had broken. Thus it became my turn to feign sleep. Soon thereafter, your teeth began to chatter and your limbs to shake, nay, your whole body shook, shook indeed so violently that the chair which you gripped with both hands thumped the floor. In vain did I put my frock coat over you— all the coats in the Austrian state could not have warmed you.

At dawn the proprietor's wife brought the breakfast: a cup of water and a slice of bread for each of us. Since I did nothing to conceal the jug, she was quick to spy the pieces. The husband, to be sure, was even quicker; in recompense for the breakage he demanded 1 gulden, 20 kreuzer. Imagine! for an earthen jug. Needless to say that I refused to pay such an exorbitant sum, nor would I be bullied.— Thus he sent for the police! In no time an officer appeared. After making your name known to him, I told the man what miseries you had suffered at the hands of the proprietor; what is more, I told him that you planned to register a complaint with the Viennese authorities. Thereat the officer laughed in my face! I was affronted, until it came out that the man had in fact heard of you. "What do you take me for, an imbecile?" he said. "Surely a composer of such renown doesn't travel by farm wagon!" Thus in the end I paid the cursed sum and we continued on our way.

The second leg of the journey proved even worse than the first, not merely because you were feverish, but because every jog along the way and every fit of coughing brought fresh pain.

We arrived here last night shortly after 9 o'clock.

———

Uncle, the maid has finally returned. Braunhofer regrets that he cannot come.

Let's send for Staudenheim.

I'll go myself this time.

———

Uncle, Staudenheim assures me that he'll visit you this evening.

———

Uncle, Councilor Breuning is waiting in the entrance hall; if it doesn't overtax you, he would like to come in for a moment.

Ludwig, are you feeling any better?

Don't tire yourself, your nephew has told me what happened at Mitterndorf. But why, if you arrived two days ago, did no one inform us?

Gerhard has been practicing as zealously as young Liszt; he is most eager to show you his new technique. But first we must find someone to look after you. According to your nephew, Dr. Braunhofer excused himself and Dr. Staudenheim failed to appear.

I've been thinking of Dr. Malfatti.

I realize that you quarreled years ago; all the same, it's my opinion that you should send for him.

Frankly I don't see why you would turn to Holz. It's unlikely he knows of a doctor that you yourself have not considered. Still, he may have heard of someone on the staff while your nephew was in the hospital.

By all means do what you think best. Meanwhile I'll arrange as soon as possible to present your nephew to the Lieutenant Field-Marshal.

Don't upset yourself; it needn't be done today, yet neither should we delay too long.

I must go now, but I'll stop by tomorrow. May God be with you, my friend.

———

No, Uncle, I didn't mislay the note to Holz; it was you who put it aside. However, I'll be glad to take down another.

Official Majesty!

I wrote to you immediately after my arrival which took place a few days ago. But the letter was mislaid. Then I fell ill, and so ill that I think it is wiser to stay in bed—Hence I shall be greatly delighted if you will visit me.

Ever your friend

BEETHOVEN

———

Maestro, I've had Professor Wawruch sent for.

No, I don't know him personally, but he is said to be one of the most skillful doctors in Vienna.

He is professor of special pathology and medical clinics at the general hospital—where, by the way, his father-in-law is the Director.

He'll come to you after dinner, about 3 o'clock.

———

Esteemed Patient, I am Prof. Wawruch, one who truly reveres your name and will do everything in his power to give you swift relief. Satis verborum

Uncle, in order to facilitate the examination I'll take down the questions.

Do you suffer from hemorroids?

When was the last bowel movement?

Take a deep breath.

Since when is the abdomen so swollen?

How often do you urinate?

Without difficulty?

The feet were never greatly swollen?

Have you ever seen blood in the stool?

Only in the sputum?

Catch your breath before you speak.

Don't speak yet.

Be calm or you will choke.

Esteemed Patient, it is clear that you are suffering from a serious in-flammation of the lungs.

Do put aside all thought of your mother and brother; the cough is not a symptom of consumption but of pneumonia.

Rest assured that it will not finish you off while Prof. Wawruch is your doctor. Your farm wagon may have brought you to death's door, but thereabouts I am the gatekeeper; as a practitioner of the medical art it is I who shall finish off the illness. Experto credite

I shall order forthwith the necessary medicines to commence a vig-orous counter-treatment.

Uncle, Dr. Wawruch says, aegrescit medendo.

I'm only joking. He said that if you don't have a bowel movement in the course of the day, you ought to be given an enema tonight.

I've already told the maid that if there is nothing by 7 o'clock, she is to fetch the barber.

Because he knows how to do it properly. What is more, he has syringes.

Wawruch found you somewhat better than yesterday. Even so, he would have you remember that every drop of urine must be saved.

So that he can gauge not only the quality but the quantity. I've given orders to buy a bedpan and a urinal. He says that the former is very comfortable and will keep you from growing so cold. He wants you to stay warm at all times. Even at night when you wake, you are to be given warm compresses. Thus someone must be near you at that time.

For a few days at most, during which the maid could sleep in here or in the entrance hall.

Since she and Sali are here at night, I see no reason for me to stay as well. Besides, you know that I promised my mother to stay with her until I leave for Iglau.

That depends on when I'm presented to the Field-Marshal.

Councilor Breuning expects to speak to him today.

———

Ludwig, the Lieutenant Field-Marshal has agreed to meet your nephew on Sunday.

In no wise precipitate, we have already delayed three months.

Assuming that all goes well, your nephew will then have to be fitted for uniforms, given a physical examination, swear the oath of service, etc. Altogether the procedure takes about a week.

Frankly I would not count on his being with you for the holidays.

But if we put it off again, I fear there will be no cadetship.

Do not give in to despair. According to Dr. Wawruch—the doctor aside, I'm able to see for myself how much better you are today.

The cases are not alike. When you nursed your mother she was dying of consumption, whereas you are being treated effectually, thank God, for pneumonia.

Naturally I remember how many weeks you sat at her bedside; the differences between you and your nephew are only too obvious. But then he is not your son.

You have indeed shown yourself a devoted father to him. I mean rather that you were your mother's *natural* son—Unless, of course, you are still disinclined to acknowledge the fact. Are you?

Not just gossip. My sister Lorchen told me that she and Wegeler wrote you last year raising the selfsame question, yet they never received a reply.

No, it's not too late; surely they would still welcome a letter.

I misunderstood you.—Too late for what?

But it was after 7 o'clock when I arrived.

I'll go and ask her.

Sali says that the maid has already gone to fetch the barber.

Vexatious, to be sure, but you'll feel much better afterwards.

At least you'll sleep more comfortably. Good night, my friend.

———

VIENNA, DECEMBER 7, 1826

My Beloved Old Friend!

Words fail me to express the pleasure which your letter and Lorchen's have afforded me. And indeed an answer should have been sent off to you as swiftly as an arrow. But on the whole I am rather slack about writing letters, for I believe that the best people know me well in any case. Often I think out a reply in my head; but when it comes to writing it down, I usually throw away my pen, simply because I am unable to write as I feel. I remember all the love which you have always shown me, for instance, how you had my room white-washed and thus gave me a pleasant surprise,—and likewise all the kindnesses I have received from the Breuning family. Our drifting apart was due to the changes in our circumstances. Each of us had to pursue the purpose for which he was intended and endeavor to attain it. Yet the eternally unshakeable and firm foundations of good principles continued to bind us strongly together.—Unfortunately I cannot write to you today as much as I should like to, for I have to stay in bed. So I shall confine myself to answering a few points in your letter.

Uncle, what Wegeler asks in effect is why you haven't defended your mother's honor.

Evidently an article in the standard encyclopedia asserts that you are a love-child who was fathered by the King of Prussia.

You say that I have been mentioned somewhere as being the natural son of the late King of Prussia. Well, the same thing was said to me a long time ago. But I have adopted the principle of neither writing anything about myself nor replying to anything that has been written about me. Hence I gladly leave it to you to make known to the world the integrity of my parents, and especially of my mother.— You mention your son. Why, of course, if he comes to Vienna, I will be a friend and a father to him; and if I can be of any use to him or help him in any way, I shall be delighted to do so.

I still possess Lorchen's silhouette. So you see how precious to me even now are all the dear, beloved memories of my youth.

As for my diplomas I merely mention that I am an Honorary member of the Royal Scientific Society of Sweden and likewise of Amsterdam, and also an Honorary Citizen of Vienna. A short time ago a certain Dr. Spiker took with him to Berlin my latest grand symphony with choruses; it is dedicated to the King, and I had to write the dedication with my own hand. I had previously applied to the Legation for permission to dedicate this work to the King, which His Majesty then granted. At Dr. Spiker's instigation I myself had to give him the corrected manuscript with the alterations in my own handwriting to be delivered to the King, because the work is to be kept in the Royal Library. On that occasion something was said to me about the Order of the Red Eagle, Second Class.

Uncle, it was ten weeks ago; I remember because we departed for Gneixendorf the following day.

All that Spiker said is that H.M. looks upon you with favor, nothing more.

It makes no difference anyway since Spiker resides in Berlin; here you would have to approach Prince Hatzfeld at the Embassy.

Surely you are in no position to prod the Prussian Ambassador.

Let's not argue the point.—Sali has made a batch of walnut cookies. Would you like some with your tea?

It would be better to have the tea first and then finish the letter. You shouldn't overtire yourself.

———

Uncle, a packet has arrived from the Prussian Embassy. Imagine! Had we not been alone yesterday, I would assume that our every word was reported to Prince Hatzfeld.

There are several letters, but doubtless you will find the one from the King of particular interest.

> BERLIN, NOVEMBER 25, 1826
>
> To the composer Ludwig van Beethoven,
>
> In view of the recognized excellence of your compositions I was greatly pleased to receive the new work which you have dedicated to me. I thank you for sending it, and send you the accompanying diamond ring as a token of my appreciation.
>
> FRIEDRICH WILHELM

Uncle, how good it is to hear you chuckle.

The ring is not enclosed.

Don't jump to conclusions; perhaps Hatzfeld is waiting to hear from you.

I still have time, provided the letter is brief.

> Sir!
>
> I send you my warmest thanks for the letters you have forwarded me. But I must ask you to be so kind as to send me the ring which

H.M. the King of Prussia has decided to give me—I am very sorry that an indisposition prevents me from receiving in person this token (which is so precious to me) of H.M.'s love of art. I should be very reluctant to have it entrusted to the hands of a stranger—At the same time I request you to inform me in a few lines whether the worshipful Ambassador would be so kind as to take charge of a letter of thanks to H.M. the King and to arrange for him to receive it.

Uncle, you are right, that would prove embarrassing. On second thought you had better wait and see if the ring arrives. Meanwhile I'll post the letter to Wegeler.

Why do you hesitate?

But you've already had a year to reflect upon the matter. Do let me post it.

Suit yourself, I must leave now.

Uncle, this just came.

GNEIXENDORF, DECEMBER 6, 1826

My dear Brother,

I am terribly sorry that you had such a miserable journey home. Had you but listened to me—However, that is water under the bridge. I do hope that you are recovering apace and will soon be enjoying better health. Unless something unforeseen occurs I shall be with you this coming Sunday.

Your devoted brother
JOHANN

No, Uncle, *tomorrow* is Sunday. Your brother will be pleased that I'm finally presented to the Field-Marshal.

Tomorrow at noon. Have you forgotten?

For Heaven's sake! On what grounds would you have me cancel it?

But you are better every day. Wawruch says that you are out of danger.

I am in no danger.

You alone hold that opinion; others don't view a career in the army as tantamount to throwing one's life away.

My friend Niemetz doesn't deserve such criticism.

He exercised no influence whatever upon me, pernicious or otherwise; I made the decision entirely on my own.

I'm not apt to change my mind.

You are mistaken if you think I'll live to regret it. On the contrary I'm impatient to be inducted so that I can get on with my life.

———

Uncle, the Field-Marshal was extremely cordial, indeed he could not have been kinder. At the end of the interview he told me to come and see him again before I leave for Iglau.

Councilor Breuning remained behind for a moment.

Although the Field-Marshal spoke in passing of the hernia operation, not a word was said about the scar.

The induction ceremony will take place on Tuesday; thereafter I'll be here another five or six days.

Unfortunately you are not well enough to come with me to the ceremony.

To Iglau! But that is impossible. Even if you regain your strength completely, Wawruch has told me that you are not to leave the house next week. Thus it goes without saying that he won't permit you to travel to Iglau.

Because it takes two days which, I need hardly remind you, entails spending the night at a village inn. It's simply out of the question.

Excuse me, there is someone at the door.

Both Breuning and your brother are waiting. Shall I fetch the Councilor first?

———

Ludwig, your brother tells me he has just arrived in town, so I'll stay but a moment.

Your nephew made a good impression on the Lieutenant Field-Marshal.

He assured me that if the boy shapes up well, he'll keep a place for him as an officer. Thus the chief hurdle has been surmounted, the rest is routine. Tomorrow Karl will be given his physical examination and the following day

I doubt that the scar will even be noticed.

Under no circumstances can his departure be postponed, neither for the holidays nor for any other reason.

You must not say such things—of course you'll see him again. In all likelihood he'll be granted a furlough in June.

Please try not to brood about it. All that matters now is for you to feel better, well enough to resume composing.

You might turn your attention to the Requiem that Wolfmayer commissioned or perhaps to the Saul and David oratorio.

That is for you to decide. But now I must leave lest I am late for dinner. Shall I send in your brother?

Brother, I'm greatly relieved to find you sitting up. Quite frankly you seem in better health than Breuning.

His face is so drawn and sallow.

Don't berate yourself for failing to speak of his health—Illness turns the attention inward.

I was glad to hear from Breuning that Karl acquitted himself favorably with the Field-Marshal—Thank Heaven, the boy is on his way at last.

Don't be concerned. Since you are indisposed I'll gladly go with him to the regimental tailor and the bootmaker, etc. Rest assured that I'll keep an eye—that is to say, my good one—on your pocketbook.

It's not a matter of stinting, yet one needn't always buy the very best cloth. Even if the difference amounts to only a gulden per ell—well, that comes to a tidy sum for two or three uniforms.

Nevertheless you have too many expenses at the moment to buy him the best.

A diamond ring!

In that case I bow to your better judgment.

Have no fear in that regard—my wife's daughter returned long since to Gneixendorf.

Of course I understand, I'm not dim-witted—He is to have the best that money can buy.

———

But Uncle, I've been combing it forward for weeks; your failure to remark on it sooner suggests that the scar is unnoticeable.

Although my appointment with the Field-Marshal is for 11 o'clock, I'm obliged to present myself to his adjutant at 10:45.

So that he can take me to the barracks and introduce me to the regimental doctor who executes the health certificate.

I believe the doctor's name is von Gulay.

I'll report the outcome this evening.

Because I have too many other things to do this afternoon.—When Wawruch comes please show him how well you walk your first day out of bed.

Damnation! Why did you do that?

Surely the regimental doctor is not going to lift up my locks to peer underneath. Now I must comb it again, and I'll be late.

———

Esteemed Patient, not only am I surprised but extremely pleased and, I may say, proud to find you up and about again. Success in the medical art, like success in composing, is never unwelcome. As you doubtless know, it was Hippocrates who coined the phrase, albeit in Greek to be sure, ars longa, vita brevis

If you were dying, I would have to agree with you that the remark is in poor taste. Since, however, you are so much better today I can only conclude that an exception has been made in Beethoven's case: et ars et vita longae

Seeing that I do not know the man, not even by reputation, I cannot express an opinion. Does this von Gutlay assert that he is at the General Hospital?

Well, that explains the matter; I count no military men among my acquaintance. Nevertheless since a physical examination requires neither diagnostic skills nor treatment, I have little doubt that von Gutlay will perform the task as competently as the next man. But why do you ask?

In progress at this moment?

Kindly do not open the window!

Because it's bitter cold outside—you will bring on a relapse!

I realize that your windows face the Alsergrund. Yet even if the glass were not steamed over and you could see the barracks, you could not possibly descry your nephew at this distance.

Let me assure you that the young man will have no difficulty in obtaining the certificate. And let me further assure you that if you continue to take the medicines which I have prescribed, distasteful though you find them, I warrant that you will fully recover. Vincit qui patitur

Your pun does me an injustice.

I shall look in tomorrow at the usual hour.

———

Uncle, von Gulay granted me the certificate; I'll be inducted tomorrow.

But it's too late to change my mind.

It's not a matter of "if" but of *when* you'll recover. You just finished telling me what Wawruch said.

He may be an asinus but everything points toward full recovery.

It's utterly insupportable to insist that you are dying.

I'm silent because you make it impossible to speak.

If I take the oath of service, I'll seem heartless or, worse, homicidal since you asssure me that it will hasten your demise; if I don't go through with it, I'll have to choose another career and start all over from scratch. I simply cannot keep postponing my life in this fashion, repeating the overture without a first act.

I haven't touched them.

Because your keys are not on the bedside table doesn't mean they are stolen.

They were in the pocket of your dressing gown. Shall I fetch the cashbox?

You needn't get up; just tell me what you want and I'll fetch it.

You are speaking in riddles.

Shall I accompany you to the entrance hall or wait here?

Please don't hurry, it's still your first day out of bed.

Had you but said that what you sought was in the credenza, I would have understood at once.

You know perfectly well I have no idea how to open the secret drawer.

If I start searching for the hidden latch, I'll be late for supper. My mother expects

A most ingenious mechanism; I would never have discovered it. But what prompts you to reveal it to me now?

Obviously they are bank shares.

Seven.

This is foolish; it goes without saying what purpose they serve and how they will be disposed of.

Well then, if you insist: they are the shares which constitute the bulk of your estate and which, presumably, I shall inherit someday.

I do indeed. From the time I was old enough to understand such things I saw how tenaciously you retained them for me; what is more, you did so despite the advice to the contrary of Dr. Bach, Breuning and your brother. I also saw how often you put my welfare ahead of your own, sacrificed your own comfort in order

True enough, the things you sacrificed were not merely comforts but necessities.

Certainly I'm appreciative. Have I not shown it many times over?

It's not a case of deserting you but of honoring my word to the Field-Marshal.

Of course I don't put him ahead of you.

Since I have no designs of any sort there is nothing for you to see through.

What object could I possibly have?

I don't see the connection between the bank shares and my entering the army.

Why do you keep saying that it will finish you off?

Premonitions aside, I still don't see the connection.

I don't deserve what you just said.

For you to characterize me as a schemer, I mean as someone who cannot wait—You malign me.

I'm in no hurry whatever to lay my hands on them. Nor do I harbor any secret hopes that

If in fact you believe that I'm acting with malice aforethought, you should cut me off here and now.

Untrue! I do *not* wish to finish you off! On the contrary I would do anything in my power

No, that is the one thing I cannot do.

But I simply *cannot* postpone the induction.

What do you mean, what will be on my head?

Have you taken leave of your senses! Please close it at once!

Never mind the barracks, you cannot stand before an open window in your night shirt.

Kindly let me close it!

I refuse to struggle with you. If you don't close it

Will you not close it!

Well and good, but it will be on *your* head!

May God preserve you, Uncle—Good night.

———

Esteemed Patient, I am terribly sorry to find you in this state. I instructed the housekeeper to fetch another quilt; it will soon allay the shivering and trembling.

She tells me that you vomited repeatedly during the night and also that you had to use the bedpan repeatedly.

Does the urinal contain all that was passed?

From your doubled-up posture I can see where the pain is most severe.

Unfortunately you are jaundiced from head to foot.

Have you had jaundice before?

How long did it persist?

The feet were not nearly this swollen yesterday; in fact you moved about with ease. How then do you account—Here is the quilt; you will soon be warmer.

Seeing that you had all but recovered yesterday, how do you account for this violent upheaval?

As a rule quarrels, however hot-tempered, do not endanger one's life.

In that case the sooner the young man departs the better; another such fit of anger will finish you off. As Horace rightly cautions us: ira furor breva est

I am not suggesting that you deserved the insults, nor that your anger was unwarranted; on the contrary your nephew's ingratitude is clear as crystal. Nevertheless you cannot put your life at risk.

In view of the jaundice and the massive swelling of the feet it is especially important to keep a close watch on the urine. Thus let me remind you again to preserve every drop.

Rest assured that no one will mistake it for Moselle. Indeed at this moment the urine is more precious than Moselle.

I shall look in again before nightfall.

———

Uncle, after what happened last night I'm not in the least surprised that you are confined to bed today.

The discoloration is unmistakable.

How unjust of you to blame me.

Was I to blame for the jaundice you suffered five years ago?

I told you last night that I would not, nay, could not postpone it.

I was inducted at noon.

If the uniforms are ready, I'll leave this coming Saturday.

By coach.

The postchaise is too expensive.

From this day on I'll be paid by the regiment. Hence all that remains to be settled is my monthly allowance from you.

It's useless to review the matter; you simply cannot accompany me to Iglau.

Since you cannot bear the sight of me, perhaps the sight of this parcel will please you. It's from the Prussian Embassy.

In all likelihood. If so, may it prove more precious than Shylock's ring. Shall I break the seal?

Alas, the fault lies not with your spectacles but with the stone; it has a decidedly reddish cast.

Who knows, it may not even be a diamond. After all, H.M. merely specified a *brilliant* ring.

I suspect that it's worth far less than Shylock paid for his. In any case you should have it appraised.

I could leave it with the court jeweler after my fitting—Unless you are afraid that I'll take a page from Jessica's book and steal it.

My impudence aside, you accused me of worse things than lying last night.

I haven't time to review what was said; I'll be late to the tailor. Do you want me to take the ring?

Suit yourself; doubtless Holz is more trustworthy than your nephew.

———

Prospero, how are you today?

Father, too, is ill. He asked me to act as his ~~ambass~~ envoy.

The doctor fears it's his liver.

You are more cheerful than I expected.

Has another ring been sent?

Goodness! I didn't notice them on the piano. I've never seen such a set of books. How many are there?

Are all forty volumes by Handel?

May I glance at one?

What a generous gift. Is it from the Prussian King?

But that's impossible; a harpmaker can't be more generous than a King.

Even so, I doubt that the books are more costly than the diamond ring.

That's easy enough to say, but where will I find someone who plays the harp "cunningly"?

Had you but mentioned the Old Testament, I would have understood.

If the speaker is Saul and he loves the youth greatly, then the harpist must be David.

I don't follow; am I to fetch the Old Testament or Handel's score of Saul?

I agree with you that the volume is beautiful, but I don't agree that the leather smells good.

I have a little English; shall I try to translate the lines for you?

Saul's first words—Well, I'm not really sure. However, they are not the words which you just spoke, of that I *am* sure.

Has an idea come for your own Saul and David oratorio?

Here is your sketchbook. Please don't let me interrupt; I'll go and report to Father.

———

Esteemed Patient, I am surprised to learn that you consider Handel the greatest composer that ever lived, superior even to J. S. Bach. When it comes to poets, spare me having to choose between Horace and Virgil.

It goes without saying that the volumes are handsome; would that I could examine them at length. However, if I am to examine the patient, I must needs remove them from the bed: they keep me at bay.

Well now, I can see that the jaundice has worsened.

Those hard knots of which you speak are nodules on the liver; the organ is distinctly swollen. Moreover, dropsy has developed: there is water in the abdomen.

As for the urine, the housekeeper tells me that you refuse to take the diuretic.

If you find it distasteful, I will have some sugar added, but you must not disregard my orders.

Because you are passing too little. When I see your nephew I shall tell him to keep a sharp eye on it—Ah! I am forgetting that he leaves tomorrow.

Postponed for how long?

Seeing that New Year's Day is still two weeks hence, I urge you not to quarrel with him; it is extremely harmful to your health—I recommend instead that you be in communion with Handel.

To that end, before I bid you adieu I will restore the volumes to the bed.

———

Uncle, is the syringe in place?

Certainly it's greased.

Then try again.

Breathe in as you insert it.

Well done—During the enema you must hold your breath, otherwise the water runs out.

Breathe naturally.

Now take a deep breath and hold it in.

Hold it fast.

Keep on holding it so that the enema works.

Now let it out.

Of course the bedpan is there—*let it out*

Voilà!

———

Brother, I fully agree with you—sell it! The most tight-fisted merchant in Krems would be ashamed to bestow such a miserable ring. If the court jeweler values it at no more than 160 gulden, so be it—let him have it at that price.

Maestro, I strongly urge you to keep it.

Brother, with all due respect to Holz, the ring is an affront.

Maestro, with all due respect to your brother, keep the ring, it is from a King.

I don't deny that you too are a king, yet not the King of Prussia.

Kings aside, Brother, it may be that we are gulled—Just think, there is no certainty that this is the ring the Prussian Ambassador received from Berlin. It's perfectly possible that Hatzfeld substituted an inferior one. In fact there is no other explanation for H.M.'s niggardliness.

Maestro, your brother's suspicion is absurd.

But you must *not* return it to Hatzfeld; that would be a worse affront to him, not to mention H.M., than the ring is to you.

Uncle, I agree with Holz. Since you cannot realize enough from the sale to make it worthwhile, keep the ring.

Maestro, it need not be decided now—sleep on it.

I don't quite follow.

Why, I sleep as you do, on a mattress.

Certainly not, my wife sleeps peacefully beside me.

As I've said before, it's customary for these things to take nine months.

———

Prospero, Father asked me to bring you this letter; it's from his brother-in-law Wegeler, in answer to yours.

How are you feeling today?

I'm sorry to hear that. Father, too, is not much better; but at least he didn't almost suffocate last night like you.

The two of you should spend the summer at a spa.

Father will probably go to Baden.

What is your objection to Baden?

I had forgotten about your nephew. In that case you and Father should go to a different spa—to Pischtein.

How ought it to be spelled?

I suppose you now agree with Father that I spell like a guttersnipe.

At least I don't play the piano like one—Excuse me a moment, there is someone at the door.

It's a certain Mr. Schindler; he seems very anxious. Doctor amo amas amat is also in the entrance hall; he is taking off his gulashes.

I'll ask Mr. Schindler to wait until the doctor leaves.

Esteemed Patient, the incident of nocturnal suffocation was brought on by the dropsy. Unfortunately a good deal of water has accumulated. Hence it presses on the diaphragm and interferes with your breathing.

Still worse, it might burst at any moment.

To guard against that danger I strongly recommend that the water be tapped.

Do not concern yourself; I have had the prudence to retain Dr. Seibert. Besides being chief surgeon at the General Hospital, he is the most distinguished practitioner of the surgical art in Vienna.

No, we are not in the least alike. For instance, when it comes to collecting his fees, Seibert is utterly dogged.

I intended no aspersion.

Let us change the subject. Naturally, you will want to obtain a second opinion. Indeed I urge you to do so.

Have you someone in mind?

One could not do better than Staudenheim. However, his aristocratic clientele may leave him little time for consultations.

By all means let us try. I shall write a brief note explaining how things stand.

There now, please have the maid deliver it at once.

But it must not wait, the matter is too urgent.

I paid little attention, except to see that there was someone else in the entrance hall.

Before I do, promise me that the note will be delivered straightway.

I shall send in Mr. Schindler.

———

Great Maestro, if indeed I knitted my brows, it's because no one prepared me for your appearance.

I'm not speaking of the jaundice but of your emaciated state.

Nothing brings me here but a heartfelt wish to see you.

From the moment you returned to Vienna I longed to come here.

I hesitated only because of Holz.

Is he not still with you?

If Holz is mostly with his wife, who serves as your amanuensis?

Yet if your nephew is soon to leave for Iglau, who will fill his shoes?

In that case perhaps you will consider taking me back—indeed I entreat you to permit me to serve you again.

But my duties with the orchestra don't occupy me night and day.

No service would strike me as too menial.

Gladly! I will take the doctor's note to Staudenheim at once.

Esteemed Patient, I will let Dr. Staudenheim speak for himself.

Celebrated Patient, I am in complete agreement with my distinguished colleague; by all means have the water tapped—the sooner the better. You will feel so much more comfortable afterwards.

Pardon me but I am here as a consultant. Kindly put the question to my honorable colleague who, in theory, is being paid for his services.

Esteemed Patient, if I chuckled, I can only ascribe it to the last entry of my distinguished colleague.

He excused himself but had to leave, owing to a previous appointment.

Fees aside, let me answer the question that you put to him. Firstly, an incision is made in the abdomen with a surgical instrument, namely, a trocar; secondly, the trocar is withdrawn leaving a tube in place; thirdly, the water is then drained off.

The whole operation, including the tapping and the dressing, will last no more than ten minutes.

It should be performed as soon as practicable.

Preferably at once, tomorrow at the latest. Shall I proceed with the arrangements?

But you cannot afford to delay. If you are pondering the pain, rest assured that Dr. Seibert will provide a goodly dose of spirits.

I am suggesting nothing of the sort; your courage is incontestable.

One moment please, Mr. Schindler wishes to have a word with you.

Great Maestro, you are wasting time. What choice is there but to go through with it?

But *it may burst at any moment!*

Esteemed Patient, I am told you now agree.

Then let us fix a time.

Better still, first thing in the morning.

Vivat Beethoven. I shall go and set the wheels in motion.

Great Maestro, since your nephew will be here later, you will be able to tell him yourself. Meanwhile I shall go and tell your brother. Presumably you don't wish his wife to be present?

Leave it to me, I shall make it clear as daylight that he is to leave the woman at home.

Councilor Breuning is still too indisposed to attend. As for Dr. Bach, I don't quite understand the wish to have your lawyer present, unless of course you plan to alter your will.

Don't be so morbid. There is no denying that death might come at any moment; however, the operation will surely set you on the road to recovery.

As you wish, I shall go first to Dr. Bach and then to your brother.

———

Esteemed Patient, thank God it is happily over.

If you feel ill you must tell me.

From this day on the sun will ascend ever higher.

Did the puncture cause you too much pain?

You bore yourself like Aeneas.

Continue to lie quietly on your side.

Kindly drink this.

A demulcent.

I am well aware that you cannot abide taking medicine; however, it is not medicine.

Lukewarm almond milk.

I warrant that you will sleep more soundly tonight.

Here is your brother who wishes to have a word with you.

In that case I shall fetch the lawyer first. But do not overtire yourself.

Worthy Friend, undoubtedly you share my feeling of relief that it is over.

In truth I don't see the similarity. Not only did the wound of Philoctetes produce a noisome stench, but it would not heal, whereas yours will heal in no time.

Believe me, you'll soon be healthy again.

The letter you wrote four years ago is not a formal will. Nevertheless it *is* a legal document. Hence it serves the same purpose.

I'll gladly draw up a new one whenever you like. Since, however, the operation is successfully over there is little need for urgency.

Is Councilor Breuning no longer Karl's guardian?

But I cannot serve as both his guardian and his trustee.

Even if you choose to exclude your brother, there are others who are suitable.

Wolfmayer for example. Besides, Breuning is likely to recover.

Only your brother and nephew are still here.

Schindler had to leave for rehearsal.

Let me first dispose of these words lest your brother take offense.

Brother, it delighted me to note that even in the face of pain you preserved your sense of humor.

I'm thinking of the moment when the surgeon withdrew the instrument and the water gushed forth; whereupon you said, "Professor, you remind me of Moses striking the rock with his staff." Did you not hear me guffaw?

A demulcent is prescribed to soothe the mucous membrane—In practice it's not unlike greasing the runners of a sledge.

Our nephew is not only here but eager to have a word with you.

Uncle, they have measured off the water; altogether it amounts to three gallons and one pint. Just imagine!

Someone ought to devise a system of dykes to control the flow.

Were you to use your finger like the Little Dutch Boy, Seibert would have apoplexy. Thank goodness the wound is bandaged.

If I'm not mistaken, you were no more than ten years old at the time.

Brother, Karl is indeed mistaken. When you and our mother went to Holland, I was five years old. Thus you were eleven.—Oh how I envied you the voyage, I mean until you told me that you almost froze to death and Mother had to tuck your hands between her thighs to prevent the frostbite.

Hardly—had it been your feet you would not have been so apprehensive of performing.

True enough, I was forgetting the foot pedals.

It's hard to believe that Mother told you the story but failed to mention that the Little Dutch Boy is a fiction.

Ah! but at the time you led me to believe that you had encountered him personally and offered to stand in his stead.

Presumably you are not alone in that—is it not every boy's fancy to plug the hole with his finger?

Need I draw a picture for you?

Uncle, let us not waste time on your brother's low humor. Another uniform is ready today.

Not until this Saturday, then I'll be obliged to pay for everything.

I don't know the reckoning.

Brother, only the full-dress uniform remains to be finished.

Rest assured that I'm keeping a strict accounting.

As soon as I've reckoned the amount, I'll inform you. Now, however, you should rest.

———

Uncle, Sali is terribly upset; evidently Wawruch holds her to blame for what happened last night.

He attributes the infection to her haste in undoing the bandage and draining off the water, whereas Sali contends that she was especially careful because the swelling was so great.

Does it feel damp just now?

You are right, there is some water oozing out.

I only wiped the area around it; the wound itself is very much inflamed.

According to Wawruch, if it's kept dry, the inflamation should subside by Christmas.

No, today is Thursday, Christmas is on Monday.

The full-dress uniform will be ready this afternoon.

I'll collect everything on Saturday, but there is still much to be done. Tomorrow your brother must come with me to pay the bills.

I've no idea, he hasn't said a word about the reckoning.

I'll ask him to stop by as soon as possible.

———

Brother, before I disclose the amount let me remind you that it was I who advocated frugality, you who insisted upon "nothing but the best."

106 gulden, 22 kreuzer for the entire lot.

Calm yourself, you have quite enough ailments without apoplexy.

You have only me to thank that it isn't *more*—why, the full-dress uniform alone

He wears it with élan—Indeed he already has every appearance of a fine cadet.

I don't follow you—forced to agree with me about what?

Then I'll go at once to the court jeweler and collect the 160 gulden.

You are mistaken—it was 160.

Absolutely certain.

As for the ring, whereabouts is it?

In that case I'll need the key to the cashbox.

I'd forgotten just how inferior the stone is—Goodness! almost any bit of quartz found along the wayside would be its equal.

We'll settle accounts tomorrow when I bring the money.

———

Brother, I'm affronted! Of course I took no commission.

Let's not quarrel—here is the jeweler's receipt in the sum of 160 gulden.

As usual your arithmetic is faulty—I owe you 53 gulden, 38 kreuzer.

So much for that! Now everything is paid for, you needn't buy him another thing.

Before I leave let me have a look at the incision.

Unforunately both the oozing and the inflammation persist.

But Christmas is the day after tomorrow.

I'm fully aware of how much you dislike Wawruch, but whom shall we send for in his stead? Braunhofer refuses to come; you had a falling out with Malfatti; Staudenheim

Then let us suffer Wawruch until Christmas Day and hope for signs of improvement.

———

Uncle, now I must ask you for some money.

Indeed you were not deceived; everything has in fact been paid for. However, I had to promise the tailor a tip in order to have the uniforms before Christmas.

But I had no way of knowing then that my departure would be postponed a second time.

Shortly after New Year's Day; the Field-Marshal hasn't yet specified the date.

By coach.

20 gulden at most.

If it seems extravagant, I can only say in my defense that the post-chaise is twice the price.

Believe me, there will be no further expenses; you have my word on that.

———

Joyous Christmas, Brother.

Granted that it's less than joyous—at least the inflammation is done with. For that we must give thanks to Doctor Full-of-himself.

It was far worse than anyone let on—Now that the crisis has passed I can tell you that Wawruch was keeping an eye out for gangrene.

That's possible, I suppose—doctors do sometimes darken the diagnosis to give themselves the appearance of a wonder-worker.

And now for a small surprise.

Joyous Christmas, Brother-in-law. To mark the holiday I made you something sweet. Behold!

It's just a simple spongecake with a milk and rum cream and some candied cherries.

Always the jokester—You have my word that it won't kill you.

Amalie is at home, but thank you for inquiring. She helped me prepare the cake and sends you warmest greetings.

Surely there is no cause to keep her under lock and key.

Have no fear for Karl. Now that he is a soldier he need only brandish his saber to protect himself from the weaker sex.

Brother, I'm afraid we must be leaving—Do enjoy the spongecake, and may your health continue to improve.

———

Uncle, the Field-Marshal was very kind again; he virtually assured me of a place as an officer if I do well. What is more, he inquired after you and offered his sincerest wishes for your good health.

I'm to leave on the 2nd of January.

Considering that I should have left ten days ago, it doesn't strike me as hasty in the least. In fact I now suspect that he postponed my departure until after the holidays in deference to you.

Why do you speak of a second operation?

I'm sorry to hear that. Has Seibert set a date?

To be with you on the 8th I'd have to turn around and come right back the moment I reach Iglau.

I simply cannot request another postponement.

As you well know, I promised to spend New Year's Eve with my mother.

It's unjust to say that I always put her first, since I plan to spend most of my last evening with you.

Have you invited other guests to join you?

In that case I can see no reason for me to dress up.

It goes without saying that you paid for it.

Indeed you are entitled to see it.

Please say no more, I shall wear the full-dress uniform.

———

Prospero, are you all alone tonight?

I suppose that Schindler is better than no one on New Year's Eve.

Father and Mother send you this bottle of sparkling wine.

I don't know how to spell champaine.

It makes no sense to spell it with g.

Do you know what I'm going to do tonight?

I'm allowed to stay up until midnight and have a glass of champagne wine.

Never before, it will be my first glass.

I fear it will go to my head.

Because that is what happened the first time I had a glass of Heuriger.

I said a dirty word.

I'd rather not repeat it.

Heavens no! It was not as dirty as that.

Please don't insist.

Please, I beg of you.

shit

Before I go back, Father, Mother and I all wish you a happy New Year and hope that the sickness will remain in the old year and that the New Year will bring you nothing but good health.

———

Great Maestro, although my toast is simple and brief, needless to say it's heartfelt: May the New Year see the complete restoration of your health.

The champagne wine is not half bad.

Apropos your health, just yesterday I urged your brother to convene a council of medical men, I mean doctors who have known your constitution longer than Wawruch and Seibert.

Staudenheim, Braunhofer and Malfatti—three men whose judgment is irrefutable.

If Braunhofer is unwilling, consult the other two.

Surely Malfatti has long since put the insult behind him.

By all means wait until it's over. However, should the second operation prove ineffectual, I strongly advise you to approach Malfatti.

Approach *a barber?* If you are in need of an enema, I'll undertake to do the job myself.

I may be an asinus, but I'll wager that you won't find a barber to shave you tomorrow for all the tea in China.

Because it's New Year's Day. You have waited three weeks, you can wait a day more.

How much are you prepared to pay the man?

In that case I'll do my best to find one.

———

Uncle, I had all but forgotten what you look like without a beard.

Well now, tell me what you think of it.

Not of the shave but of the uniform; you haven't said a word.

Apart from the tip, I'm glad that it pleases you.

Unfortunately there is no way around it; if I hadn't tipped him, it wouldn't fit me properly.

True enough, but what matters is that it does fit.—Now try to finish up the pancakes so that Sali's feelings won't be hurt.

Even so, do try; you hardly touched the soup.

Without the beard it's obvious how much weight you've lost. Let's hope that your appetite improves in the new year.

All the same I shall worry about you while I'm away.

But that's a different matter; there is no reason for you to worry about me.

The training is merely routine. Believe me, I shall be in no danger at Iglau.

Please don't turn your face to the wall, not tonight, I mean my last night in Vienna.

Would you like me to step out a moment?

Then tell me, if you will, what makes you grieve so.

That is foolish, of course you will see me again.

Premonitions aside, the moment I'm granted a furlough, you have my word

If that is not your chief concern, what is?

Who will take care of me *when?*

I don't follow you—Do you mean who will take care of me after you leave this life?

Why then I'll take care of myself, naturally.

You must not worry about such things. Surely if I'm old enough to serve in the military, I'm old enough

Only in your eyes am I still a boy.

I realize that I haven't attained my majority; nevertheless I am 20 years old.

Dear Uncle, please don't worry; somehow I shall find my way.

I don't use "Father" for the simple reason that I am not your son.

On the contrary you have treated me with devotion and unstinting generosity. For that you have my deepest gratitude.

It goes without saying that you also have my love.

Why do you disparage a nephew's love? Is it ipso facto inferior to a son's?

What matters is the sentiment, not how I address you.

Firstly, if you were in truth dying, you may be sure that I would stay; secondly, in no wise am I deserting you, I am simply doing my duty.

But even if I were your natural son, I

By no stretch of the imagination am I your "bodily son"—Yet even if that were the case, I should be obliged to leave for Iglau.

As for filial piety, forgive my impudence but when your own father died you did not return for his funeral.

Nor did I say that you beat me. Why do you speak of beatings?

Please don't remove your night shirt. I would hardly be able to see the bruises at any rate, inasmuch as your father laid those blows upon you fifty years ago.

Naturally you continued using that form of address; in spite of the blows he was still your father.

I don't deny that you are mine—in all but body.

Nothing makes me hesitate; if you wish, I'll gladly call you Father.

I'm not aware that I rubbed my temple.

Of course I don't hold you to blame for what happened, at least not in retrospect. After all, the wound was self-inflicted.

Why do you grieve again—don't, I entreat you.

What reproaches?

But they are long forgotten. Besides—Who knows, perhaps I deserved your reproaches.

Please now, no more grieving.

Since there is hardly a scar to speak of, I would prefer not to.

If it doesn't concern the scar, why do you ask me to lower my head?

Ought I to go out to the flock like Jacob and fetch a goatskin?

Forgive me, I was only joking. In truth I would welcome, nay, cherish your blessing.

O thank you—I don't—I—thank you.

Indeed I'm not too old to be kissed.

And you, are you too old?

Rest assured that I shall write you regularly.

Now I must say good-bye. May the New Year bring you full recovery and the glorious completion of your Saul & David oratorio.

Farewell, ~~Uncl~~ my dear Father.

———

5

GREAT Maestro, not only am I flattered by your willingness to take me back, but I am eager to prove myself worthy of your trust.

Is Dr. Bach's address unchanged?

VIENNA, WEDNESDAY, JANUARY 3, 1827

Esteemed Friend!

Before my death I declare that Karl van Beethoven, my beloved nephew, is the sole heir to all my property, including, chiefly, seven bank shares and whatever cash may be available—Should the laws prescribe alterations pertaining to this bequest, then try to turn them so far as possible to my nephew's *advantage*—I appoint you *his trustee* and ask you together with his guardian, Councilor von Breuning, to be a father to him—May God preserve you—A thousand thanks for the love and friendship you have shown me—

LUDWIG VAN BEETHOVEN

Great Maestro, are there no provisos?

Some stipulation which would prohibit *the mother* from laying her hands on anything.

You would do well to ask Dr. Bach if "sole heir" suffices. As for your nephew, would it not be wise to impose certain limitations?

On his behavior, naturally. Considering his love of gambling and café life, I venture to say he'll run into debt unless you rein him in.

A mistake about what?

By no means have you made a mistake where *I* am concerned.

Forgive me, in future I'll keep my views of your nephew to myself.

I have already said that I'll keep them to myself, what more do you wish? Come now, do relent.

I beg you to relent.

But if you send me packing, who will you find to take my place? Surely not your worthy brother.

You cannot be in earnest.

But young Breuning is hardly capable of

As you wish, I'll fetch him for you now. Before I do, however, you may rest assured that in all Vienna, not to mention the whole Imperial State, there is not a single schoolboy, no matter how bright (which this one is certainly not), who has the requisite skills, patience and, I may say, fortitude to take my place.

———

Prospero, how are you feeling?

Father, too, is about the same.

He is well enough to read a letter.

I don't know if he is well enough to reply.

I'll tell him that you would welcome his opinion, if it's no trouble.

I left Schindler in the entrance hall.

I'll send him to you.

———

Well, Great Maestro, are you satisfied with your new amanuensis?

Oh? And may I ask the nature of your reservation?

I'm not at all surprised, few children nowadays are able to spell; they think only of dancing and playing billiards. Yet if young Breuning won't do, who is to take my place?

Thank you, I'm pleased to resume my duties.

The letter is on the bedside table.

In that case I'll retrieve it from Breuning after dinner and ask if there is a reply.

———

Dearest Friend!

I am still too weak to write you at length, but I think that a few candid words from the heart should be spoken. Since through Gerhard you have asked me to read the letter to Dr. Bach, I have done so and return it to you for the time being with the following observations: that you name Karl as heir in the event, which I hope is far off, that you leave this life, is appropriate considering your way of thinking and what you have already done for him. But up until now

Karl has shown himself to be very reckless, and one doesn't yet know how his character will develop. Thus I would recommend that for his own good and for his future security you limit his power to dispose of capital either for life or at least for a few more years, until he turns 24 years, the age of his majority. In any case he would have enough annual income on hand and the limitation would protect him from the consequences of reckless actions before he reaches maturity. Speak of this with Dr. Bach from whom I should think a visit would be helpful. He will arrange everything in the simplest way; I would welcome the opportunity to talk with you or with Dr. Bach about my observations, for I fear that a mere time limitation will not keep Karl from contracting debts which he would only have to pay subsequently from his eventual inheritance.

I embrace you warmly.

STEPHAN

———

Worthy Friend, although I agree with Councilor Breuning that Karl's behavior last year was reckless, I'm not convinced that you should limit his freedom to dispose of the capital. From your letter to me it's clear that you have no such object in mind. Hence I would advise you to follow your heart and impose no limitations.

The notion of controlling Karl's behavior from beyond the grave strikes me as harsh. What happened last year was not extraordinary: many young men of Karl's age are inclined to play billiards, gamble and even to attempt suicide—God be thanked he did not succeed. Besides, I suspect that such behavior is now behind him.

I realize that you had the highest hopes for him, yet he is not without merit—indeed he is altogether intelligent, affable and conscientious. Added to that, he is devoted to you.

I truly doubt that he is more devoted to her.

The only way to prevent his mother from receiving any portion of the capital is to hold it in trust; therewith you could stipulate that the interest will go to Karl for the rest of his life and the principal pass to his legitimate off-spring after his death.

You need not decide the matter now, there will be plenty of opportunity

Do not despair; the grim reaper is still far off.

A trocar and a scythe are hardly equivalent. Has the surgeon said when it will be performed?

Since tomorrow is Friday, it will likely be sometime next week.

No more of that. Not only will you survive the operation, but you will go on to finish your tenth symphony.

It's no trouble, believe me. If I'm obliged to lecture on the day of the operation, then I'll come here immediately afterwards.

May God be with you, my friend.

———

Brother, I cannot help but agree with Breuning.

I'm surprised that Dr. Bach holds the opposite view—No doubt that is because he has had so few dealings with our nephew.

I'm thinking of neither the gambling debts nor the goings-on at Gneixendorf, but of Karl's devotion to his mother—Have you considered the possibility that he might predecease her—God forbid!

Nevertheless, now that he is in the military there is no telling what might happen. In my opinion you ought to create a trust.

Well, if Dr. Bach said the same, that should settle it.

What others? You've already consulted with everyone worthwhile—everyone, that is to say, but Wolfmayer.

What on earth for? Holz is a connoisseur of wines not of business dealings.

Well and good, if I happen to see him, I'll mention

But surely it can wait until Monday.

In that case I'll stop by the Chancellery now and ask him to visit you tomorrow.

———

Prospero, how are you this morning?

Has your stomach become smaller?

Then the surgeon shouldn't delay.

Has your appetite improved?

By now you should be eating meat.

Have you been given an enema?

You should be given more of them.

Have you finished reading Walter Scott?

Would you like to read Schiller?

Perhaps you'd like Sommer's travel sketches.

Doctor amo amas amat has just arrived; he is taking off his coat.

Don't speak so loudly or he'll hear you. Father, too, considers him a bungler.

I must go now. I'll bring you the Sommer tomorrow.

Esteemed Patient, be so good as to turn over.

But if you turn your back on me, I cannot examine you.

Unless I examine you, I cannot consult with Dr. Seibert.

Without consultation we cannot determine when next to tap the water.

Tomorrow seems premature; I am still inclined to wait.

Because the moment it is tapped, the water reaccumulates. Besides, this cold rainy weather only aggravates the dropsy. Thus I think it best to delay as long as possible.

Since the tappings are in no wise a cure, you are not incorrect to call them a palliative, albeit a necessary one. Nor can I deny the possibility of future tappings.

Your argument is indisputable. The Romans, as you doubtless know, deemed logic the art of arts. I may, therefore, reverse my judgment and recommend that Dr. Seibert perform the operation this coming week.

———

Great Maestro, for weeks and weeks I've tried to persuade your know-it-all brother to call in Malfatti for consultation, but to no avail. Yet as much as I value Malfatti, you must not lose faith in Wawruch; after all, he has done a great deal already.

In spite of your antipathy to him, Wawruch is regarded as an able man, esteemed and appreciated by his students. Although I can't speak from experience, I myself have considerable confidence in him.

Even so he has a thorough understanding of his profession, that is well known.

For him to speak of the *possibility* of a third operation is quite different from his regarding it as inevitable. Don't always look on the dark side.

Since there is time before my rehearsal let us deal with the letter to your nephew.

My dear Son!
   It is clear now that the two learned gentlemen have a second operation up their sleeve; all that remains to be decided upon is the date.

Great Maestro, excuse me a moment.

Sali says that Holz is here. Oddly enough, I saw your Mr. Holz just yesterday and gave him a good piece of my mind.

Because I heard from someone that he doesn't like my coming here. I called him to account for that.

Holz insisted that he had said nothing of the kind and felt no jealousy where I am concerned. Further, he told me that he must divide his time between his office, his lessons and his bride; hence he cannot come to see you. Yet lo and behold, here he is! Clearly the man is not to be trusted.

I told him to wait, naturally.

How was I to know that you had sent for him? I'll fetch him at once.

Maestro, forgive me for neglecting you these last few weeks, but lately I find myself without a moment to spare.

Would that my duties were confined to the bedroom. Unfortunately they take me to the office, the quartet, lessons, etc. Nor do I see any respite in sight.

Great Maestro, far from "lurking about," I am waiting for you to finish the letter to your nephew.

If you wish me to step out for a moment, you need only say so.

Indeed I have no objection, so long as you understand that if I leave for the day, the letter will not—Or do you plan to have Mr. Holz do the job in my stead?

I take you at your word. Meanwhile I shall wait to hear from you. Good day.

Goodness, Maestro, seldom have I seen such a puffing of the breast, such searching looks and darting glances—Yet you surely didn't send for me just to goad Schindler.

Although I know there is a secret drawer, I have no idea of its where-abouts.

I can imagine why you might wish to keep your brother in igno-rance, but not why you wish to reveal it to me. Seeing that Breuning is your closest friend, wouldn't

I hadn't heard he was ill. In that case I'll bear the burden, albeit re-luctantly, providing that you promise to live another twenty years.

Esteemed Patient, owing to Dr. Seibert's customary skill the second operation is now successfully behind you.

Do you still feel much pain?

Aurelius himself could not have borne it more stoically.

The water was clearer today, a good sign.

Twice as much as last time, almost six gallons.

If another operation should become necessary, I shall certainly not look for twelve. Now please drink this.

Regardless of how much you hate medicine, it is critically important to take it after an operation. Vincit qui se vincit

But it is for your own good.

Sometimes I wonder which of us is the doctor, which the patient.

Do try to rest quietly.

Great Maestro, now that it's over, I must confess that I often feared you would choke before they made up their minds when to operate.

I kept it to myself because I didn't wish to dampen your spirits.

I praised Wawruch for the same reason.

He had no right to remark on future tappings. Where will it end!

There is only one answer: your brother must call in Malfatti.

Then take it upon yourself. Let us draft a note forthwith.

My dear Malfatti,

    As you may have heard I have been confined to bed with dropsy since early December and in this connection have just undergone a second operation. Every day I hope to see an end to this trying illness, yet every day it persists. Unfortunately the doctor in attendance, a certain Professor Wawruch, has no prior knowledge of my constitution. Why, in the last five weeks alone I have been compelled to empty 75 bottles of some witches' brew and to swallow God only knows how many different powders. He is ruining me with overmuch medicine! Although I have done my best to tolerate his treatment, frankly I have lost all confidence in the man. Thus I beg of you to come to my aid as soon as possible—Believe me, it is a matter of life and death.

Your most devoted

BEETHOVEN

Great Maestro, I'll take it to him at once.

Great Maestro, I bring you back a disappointing reply.

He didn't even condescend to write it. "Say to Beethoven that as a master of harmony he ought to know that I, too, must live in harmony with my colleagues."

No mention was made of old wounds, only of his colleagues, naturally. Like all members of the medical profession, Malfatti's first allegiance is to his colleagues.

Apart from his cultivated suavity, I found him quite severe and glacial. Indeed despite his southern heritage, he has every appearance of the Swiss. Perhaps he hails from the Italian side of the Alps.

I understand your bitter disappointment, yet tears are premature.

Because he didn't close the door completely.

Surely his unwillingness to take Wawruch's place doesn't imply an unwillingness to *consult* with him.

Then let us try again, with fewer words and more flattery.

My dear Malfatti,
    As the pre-eminent master of harmony I bow my knee to you, the pre-eminent master of the medical art, and ask only that you introduce an element of counterpoint *in consultation with* Dr. Wawruch.
    With deepest respect I remain ever your most devoted
BEETHOVEN

———

Great Maestro, I bring you glad tidings! Malfatti agrees to consult with Wawruch and the others the day after tomorrow.

Goodness, tears when he won't come and tears when he will.

True enough, there is every reason now to look for real improvement.

———

Esteemed Patient, my distinguished colleagues and I have concluded our consultation.

Seeing that Dr. Malfatti is an old friend of yours, he naturally appreciates far better than we your idiosyncrasies, in particular your decided taste for spirits. Thus I shall step aside for the moment while you learn from him the novel course of treatment he has hit upon.

Beethoven, you are more than kind. Still, you must not entertain such lofty expectations. In spite of my reputation for performing miracles, I am not Aesculepius.

No apologies are necessary. Although we have not exchanged a word in ten years, I bear you no ill-will. Do keep in mind that I am from the venerable city of Lucca, not from vengeful Corsica. Besides, ten years ago you had just been appointed your nephew's guardian and had your hands full—Indeed from what I am told they are still so.

It is Dr. Wawruch's opinion that much of your illness is due to the mental distress your nephew has inflicted upon you.

Not only at present but from the start; and indeed I thoroughly agree with him.

Seeing that I am pressed for time let me come to the point. Do you still enjoy a good Moselle?

Then let us do away with all those powders and medicine bottles that you so detest. In their place I have arranged for you to be given a very simple recipe: a daily glass of frozen punch.

By no means am I joking.

Nothing whatever, only the punch. Yet note well, you are not to drink more than one glass a day. If you abuse my orders, as is your wont, rest assured that you will come to grief. What is more, you are never to drink it in its liquid form, only frozen. In addition I have given orders for the abdomen to be rubbed with ice-cold water.

The object, in brief, is to tone up your digestive organs; at present they are utterly worn-out.

You will start the regimen today.

No, no, that is out of the question.

Quite simply because I have not the time to take on another patient.

Unfortunately the same is true of my assistants, all of us are overtaxed.

You should have thought of that ten years ago.

I cannot stay another moment, so let it be. If possible I shall look in on you occasionally. Meanwhile you are perfectly safe in Dr. Wawruch's hands.

———

Dear Schindler,
    Miracles! Miracles! Miracles! The highly learned professors are

both defeated. Only through Malfatti's practice shall I be saved! It is necessary that you come to me for a moment before noon.

B.

Great Maestro, the transformation is indeed a miracle. Not only has Malfatti toned up your digestive tract, but he has restored your spirits overnight.

The whole night through, without waking even once?

That in itself is a miracle.

How heartening it is to see the fire in your eyes again, to hear you speak again of your Saul & David oratorio.

Come now, it was Malfatti who prescribed the treatment—is that not enough?

Don't make so much of his taking you back as a patient; to all intents and purposes *you are his patient*.

I'll go to him if you insist, yet would it not be shrewder to wait and let him come to you, as he promised.

Even if he sends one of his assistants, at least the man will offset Wawruch.

Well and good, if Malfatti doesn't visit within the week, rest assured that I will go to him.

But haven't you already had your glass for the day?

In that case you cannot have another.

Benefits aside, you simply cannot have a second glass of punch.

I'll thank you not to say that. The Spirit that Denies indeed! If anything, I am your guardian angel.

———

Great Maestro, it seems that the busy cadet found time at last to
write.

IGLAU, JANUARY 13, 1827

My dear Father,

I have received your letter written by Schindler; I ask only that in
future you include the date so that I can estimate the speed of the
post. As for the state of your health, I am so happy to know that you
are in good hands; I, too, had some misgivings about the treatment
of your former (or perhaps still present?) doctor; I hope that from
now on all will go well.

I wrote to Councilor Breuning some days ago and indicated the
things that I still need. I would have written you directly, but I
wanted not to tire you. No doubt the Councilor will attend to everything in the best way.

You wish to know my circumstances in detail. My captain is
a thoroughly cultured man with whom I expect to get along very
well. I share a nice room with the company sergeant-major, a very
fine young man.—There is no such thing as an officer's mess here;
everyone goes to eat where he pleases. To economize I have already
changed my eating place several times, but now a common mess
for cadets is to be set up—if it is ever finished. Meanwhile in the
evening everyone leaves the barracks to look for a place to eat. I have
an orderly who takes care of me and receives 1 gulden a month,
not counting small outlays for white lead and chalk to clean the
uniforms. Washing also comes to a few gulden, if one wants it really
clean. There is a theater here, too, to which I go with the captain's

permission.—These are more or less the ordinary circumstances that I am able to report at present.

Of the things that I requested from Councilor Breuning and still need, the captain cannot supply anything without authorization, naturally; therefore I ask you to mention it to the Councilor. And if you would send me something extra to cover the unavoidable expenses that I have already explained to him, it would be most kind. What is more, I depended upon receiving my pay from the day that I enrolled (Dec. 12, 1826), but this has not happened because the enrollment roster remains in Vienna. Thus I must still watch every penny.

In conclusion one more request. A first lieutenant who loves music and especially your works, plans to perform the Pianoforte Concerto in B flat (Op. 19) at his quarters this week. However, by accident the flute part has been lost, and so he has turned to me. Hence may I ask you to arrange for the part to be sent to me as soon as possible.—Do not worry about my address; I receive letters in care of the regimental adjutant.—Write to me again very soon. I embrace you with all my heart. My regards to the Councilor.

Your loving son

KARL

P.S. Do not think that the little privations to which I am now subjected have made me malcontent. On the contrary, rest assured that I am happy here, and regret only that I am so far away from you. But with time that, too, will change.

As you see, I have treated myself to a seal with my name.

Great Maestro, it is one thing to watch every penny and quite another to treat oneself to theater and a name seal, etc.

That is for you to decide. However, before you send him anything, you ought to review your own accounts.

I am not suggesting that you are in arrears, except where Wawruch and Seibert are concerned, yet neither is the cashbox overstuffed. Besides, you have no way of knowing how much Malfatti will charge you for his services.

He may have come to you as your friend, but don't assume for a moment that as your doctor he'll depart without his fee.

I won't wager with you simply because I don't wish to take your money.

You stint yourself and yet would send your nephew 20 gulden!

Not even 10, seeing that you have no idea how he plans to spend it.

In that case I have nothing more to say. I'll do my best to hunt down the flute part this afternoon and post it together with the money in the morning.

———

Esteemed Patient, is the neck merely stiff or is there pain?

I am somewhat confused. Are you speaking of Saul and the Witch of Endor, or of Aeneas and the Sybil of Cumae? It would seem that you compound the two.

Confound the two?

Medical practitioners? I don't follow you.

If one is not to tell it in Gath, then it must be Saul.

Ah! But therein lies the confusion: Samuel is summoned up by the

Witch of Endor, whereas Aeneas is directed down to the underworld by the Sybil.

He descends in order to behold his father—ire ad conspectum cari genitoris et ora

Mother? In that case you have confused Aeneas with Odysseus; it is Odysseus who descends in search of his mother.

Plutarch?

Please excuse me for a moment.

Your housekeeper informs me that you took more than one glass of punch yesterday, nay, not only yesterday but the day before.

Do not blame her; the moment you mentioned your neck pain and I heard you wander in your speech, I suspected something of the sort.

I shall put it to you plainly: if you continue to abuse Dr. Malfatti's orders, I fear that it is Beethoven who will end in the underworld.

———

JANUARY 19, 1827

My Great Maestro!

Since I have a rehearsal today at half past eight and cannot possibly afford to miss it, I must report in writing the upshot of my second visit to Malfatti.

He will come to you this morning at half past nine. Knowing perfectly well that Wawruch has a lecture until ten, I told Malfatti that we were also inviting the Professor to come at half past nine. In order that we don't get into a pickle you need only say to Malf. that you did not learn until today that the Professor's lecture prevented him from coming before ten. For his part Malf. has a meeting in the city at ten; thus you finally have your opportunity to speak to him alone.

Since, however, the past still rankles him somewhat, I would ask you to patch things up completely; why, only today he gave me to understand that he could not forget your "calculated offense," as he called it.—Some artful words from you will put everything to rights and restore the status quo.

Around two o'clock I shall have the honor of being with you again. Meanwhile summa cum reverentia

Your obliging

ANT. SCHINDLER

———

Beethoven, both the diarrhea and the Kolik are brought on by the cold fomentations—I shall give orders to discontinue them at once. However, the rest of your complaints, namely, the neck pain, the rattle when you breathe, the hoarseness, the stupor etc., those are of your own making. Thus I shall also give orders to cancel the frozen punch.

Because you are abusing the prescription.

On the contrary it is clearly harming you.

Nonsense, you have never done as you were told and never will. Of all the patients I have treated in my lifetime you are the most unruly, to say nothing of the most offensive.

Was it not offensive to represent me, the pre-eminent physician in Vienna, as not only stupid but dishonest?

Rubbish, you retailed it all over town!

The charge of stupidity was easily dismissed. But what of the trumped-up dishonest? People had no idea what you were aiming at, of what I was accused. Nor, God knows, did I. How dared you defame me in that fashion!

Kindly spare me talk of friendship—In what way *dishonest*?

In what way I ask!

Answer me! Did you suppose that I was after your gold ducats from the Philharmonic Society?

Claptrap! The man came all the way from London to be treated by Malfatti, not to chat with Beethoven. Your name was utterly unknown to him until it passed my lips. Indeed it was only through my good office that he even heard your music played.

So much then for my alleged dishonesty. Yet even that I might have stomached, had you but spared me your final affront.

Is it possible to forget such a filthy epithet?

The word you used was *wily*— "wily Italian."

In that case I'll enlighten you—Turks are wily, Italians are ingenious!

Nettled understates it, I was enraged! I cursed and damned your miserable heart! Had you been near me, I would have cut your throat! In lieu of that, I swore by the Almighty that I would never speak to you again, never tip my hat to you, never acknowledge in any way that you had been born—So, as you see, I have broken my holy vow by coming here.

Never mind how close we once were, on no account do I wish to patch things up.

My object, indeed my sole object in coming here was to settle old scores.

I shall do as I said, stop by from time to time; if you expect more, you will be sorely disappointed.

Very well, the prescription will be maintained, but only so long as you obey my orders. And don't for a moment assume that Malfatti can be hoodwinked by the likes of you—a crude double-dealing Austrian!

———

Esteemed Patient, although the testes are somewhat retracted, there is no cause for alarm. Of more immediate concern is the blood you observed.

And prior to that was there blood in the stool?

Only a trace?

Is your appetite still so poor?

I begin to suspect that the seat of the trouble is the liver.—But the liver aside, it is now clear that another operation is needed.

Naturally, not only have I discussed the matter with your Dr. Malfatti, but also with Dr. Seibert, and both agree that it must be performed.

To the best of my knowledge the prescription is still in force—you will continue to receive one glass per day. However, I should tell you in candor that the frozen punch is not having the desired effect.

On the contrary, if it were, there would be no need for a third operation.

Come now, there is no reason to hang your head. In all the world there could not be a more distinguished group of doctors than those assembled here for you. If any practitioners of the art can bring about a happy result, we can.

Trust in us.

———

Great Maestro, Wawruch gave me to understand that Seibert has already reported the results to Malfatti.

Now that the operation is over, one would think that Malfatti himself could find the time to look at the liver and belly.

There has been no word from him. However, Seibert plans to examine you once more today.

Perhaps he wishes to see if the fluid is passing through the liver. Evidently the liver is the key to the whole business.

To be on the safe side Seibert should be sent for at 5 o'clock.

For one thing to inform you of his findings, for another to give Malfatti the most thorough report possible.

Now for a different matter—A note has come from the soprano Schechner; it so happpens that her father, too, once had dropsy.

The point is that the man was ultimately *cured*.

I have no idea. In any case I said that I would stop by and see the mother this afternoon.

If she tells me anything pertinent, I'll report back to you.

———

Great Maestro, I have just come from Madame Schechner's. Not only was her husband cured, but he was over 70 at the time!

She wanted to make certain that your doctors were familiar with the remedy.

Some sort of steam bath decocted from a head of cabbage, two hand-fuls of caraway seeds and three handfuls of hayseed.

Granted that it smacks of Macbeth, yet it proved effective in her hus-band's case. Besides, the remedy was prescribed by a Royal Physi-cian.

Let us leave no stone unturned. I'll go to Malfatti at once and sound him out on the matter.

———

Great Maestro, Malfatti was quick to recognize the prescription. Apparently it was used by a certain Dr. Harz who was indeed the Royal Physician to the late King of Bavaria.

Seeing that the internal medicine has proved ineffectual, Malfatti is willing to try the prescription. However, he would vary some of the ingredients—or, as he put it, he is "quite ready to perform variations on a theme by Dr. Harz."

He'll come to you tomorrow morning.

Brother, of course the remedy is known to me—why, I have known of it since my apothecary days in Linz.

Who is Harz?

I must confess that I am unfamiliar with his music.

Harz aside, the treatment has been employed for years as a kind of home remedy—the dry hayseed is supposed to make you perspire and have a beneficial effect. My only doubt in your case is whether your system is ready for a steam bath so close on the heels of the operation.

Malfatti's assistant has already put in place the hayseed and hot water jugs.

At present the man is spreading birch leaves over the jugs. When that is done you will step into the bath-tub, be covered with a bed sheet (but for your head, naturally) sit down on the birch leaves and—voilà the treatment!

The first bath is to last no longer than half an hour.

You have every reason to be hopeful—Malfatti himself is most hopeful.

Naturally, all of us are hopeful and pray for a good result.

That was the assistant to say that everything is now ready.

Great Maestro, the girl will put a wooden bowl under the bed so that the fluid won't run all over the floor.

Unfortunately there is no more straw in the house to fill the other mattress; all the straw is fouled. The other one will be filled this evening and you may use it tonight.

The stove could not be hotter. When she comes with the bowl I'll tell—But here she is.

I told her to bring you another blanket.

In truth Malfatti failed to return. However, the assistant did; also your brother looked in again while you slept. He insists that he forewarned you of the bloating.

As I understand it, the steam bath did not work because you had just been tapped two days ago and were completely drained of fluid. Thus instead of making you perspire, it had the opposite effect: your body soaked up the steam like a block of salt.

No need to fret, the treatment has been cancelled.

Since nothing was said to the contrary, I assume that the frozen punch is still prescribed.

Apropos of the punch, Moselle costs money, especially when visitors such as Holz help themselves freely. Fuel costs money, the more so because of the heavy snowfall; why, even little things such as straw and hayseed cost money. Above all else, doctors cost money.

Unfortunately when the assistant returned he minced no words about Malfatti's fee. Moreover no opportunity passes without Wawruch mentioning his "honorarium"; and Seibert did the same on Friday.

One moment please while she spreads the blanket.

Is that not better?

I have been thinking that perhaps you should consider selling a bank share, I mean only until such time as you are able to work again.

Needless to say that they will go to your nephew eventually, but for the moment they still belong to you.

In that case how do you propose to pay for your expenses?

Well and good, but who? Have you someone in mind?

Frankly I can't think of anyone you might approach for funds.

Gerhard just came in—perhaps the boy's father will be able to suggest someone.

I must take my leave now. I'll come again tomorrow at the usual time.

Prospero, was the steam bath a success?

I'm sorry to hear that. Still, you mustn't lose confidence in Malfatti. He is your best doctor.

If they had had the sense to cover the mattress with oil cloth, it wouldn't be soiled.

I'll bring you some oil cloth tomorrow.

Don't concern yourself, I'll trust you for the money. Meanwhile what can be done to cheer you? Would you like to read Plutarch?

Would you like to study a volume of Handel's works?

I'm flattered, but what did I say that was smart?

Sir smart?

I thought that the Englishman who sent you the books is named Stumpff.

Then what has Sir Smart to do with Handel?

I don't see the connection between my being smart and Sir Smart being a member of the Filharmonic Society.

Oh how I hate words that begin with *ph*!

Well, at least I've cheered you. Now I have to leave.

Have you forgotten that today is Sunday? Father is at home.

I'm sure that he'll find time. I'll go and ask him.

———

Ludwig, it's hard to believe that you would even entertain such a thought.

To represent yourself as *wanting* to either Stumpff or Smart—why, it would be a bold-faced lie, to say nothing of immoral.

For the simple reason that you own seven bank shares.

In that case why not approach your brother? Surely he is in a position to assist you.

Frankly I never thought you would stoop so low as to ask for a handout.

Call it what you like, it comes to the same thing.

Vienna may not have always appreciated your music, but she has always supported you and, better still, with no strings attached. For you to turn now to London strikes me as—well, unseemly.

Consult with Dr. Bach or Wolfmayer, consult with your brother or Holz or even Schindler; I doubt that you will find anyone who disagrees with me.

True enough, yet my sole object in being harsh is to persuade you to reconsider.

Do weigh it carefully.

———

Great Maestro, seldom have I seen you so gloomy.

Of course your bills must be paid, there is no gainsaying that. And as for your friends, among whom I am proud to count myself, surely this won't be the first time, nor doubtless the last, that you go against their wishes.

If writing Stumpff will lift your spirits, by all means let us get on with the letter.

VIENNA, FEBRUARY 8, 1827

My very dear Friend!

My pen is quite unable to describe the great pleasure afforded me by the volumes of Handel's works which you have sent me as a gift—to me, a royal gift!—This present has even been mentioned in the Viennese papers, and I am sending you the notice. Unfortunately since December 3rd I have been confined to bed with dropsy. You can imagine the situation to which this illness has reduced me. Usually

I live entirely on the profits of my intellectual work and manage to earn everything for the support of myself and my Karl. But unfortunately for the last two and a half months I have not been able to write a single note.

My income suffices only to pay my half-yearly rent, leaving me a few hundred gulden. Bear in mind too that the end of my illness is not by any means in sight. Nor do I know when it will be possible for me to soar again through the air on Pegasus in full flight! Physician, surgeon, everything has to be paid for—

I well remember that several years ago the Philharmonic Society wanted to give a concert for my benefit. It would be helpful for me if they would decide to do so now. Perhaps I might still be rescued from the poverty with which I am now faced. I am writing to Sir Smart about this. And if you, dear friend, can contribute something to this object, do please come to an agreement with Sir S. A letter about this is being written to my old friend Moscheles as well. And if all my friends combine, I believe it will be possible to do something for me in this matter.

In regard to supplying Handel's works to His Imperial Highness the Archduke Rudolph, I cannot say anything definite yet. But I will write to him in a few days and draw his attention to this suggestion.

I thank you again for your splendid gift. Please make use of me, and if I can serve you in any way in Vienna I shall be delighted to do so—Once more I appeal to your philanthropic feelings in regard to my situation which I have described to you in this letter. I send you my best and most cordial wishes and my warmest compliments.

> With kindest regards, your
>
> BEETHOVEN

Great Maestro, as for the letter to Sir Smart, I'll simply copy this one and replace the parts about Handel with some niceties about Smart's visit here the summer before last. That done, I'll send it to your nephew to translate into English.

If I post the letter today it will reach Iglau by Saturday.

Allowing a week for the job, he should have it back to you by the 20th.

I'll copy it now.

———

Prospero, you seem in better spirits today.

A present from whom?

May I see it?

It's very nice. But why would an artist bother to make a lithograph of such a humble house?

I don't assume anything of the kind. You, for instance, are a great man, yet I happen to know that you were not born in a palace.

Is the great man a composer?

Then the house must be Handel's birthplace.

I didn't realize that Haydn's family was so poor.

I'm sure that Father will know of a framer. Shall I take it home with me?

Don't concern yourself, I'll be very careful with it.

———

Great Maestro, do try to apply your mind to something other than your nephew. As you know, I'm not his staunchest advocate; still, even if he set to work the moment your letter arrived, he could not have returned the translation—today is only the 15th.

You mustn't assume that you are out of his heart, if for no other reason than that he is still entirely dependent upon your pocketbook.

Don't fret about it, he surely has not forgotten you.

Nonsense! No one has forgotten you.

That is absurd! You are anything but a forgotten man. Why, just yesterday Diabelli brought you a lithograph, and the previous day Haslinger was here. All sorts of people are eager to visit you; if they hesitate it's only because they don't wish to intrude.

Wolfmayer for one, Hüttenbrenner for another. I don't know how many times Hütten. has asked me if he might bring Schubert.

But I myself have often told you how much Schubert reveres your work and worships you.

Indeed I just happen to have a collection of his songs with me today.

approximately 60

By no means all, thus far he has written well over 500.

Never mind the number, wait until you discover their wonder.

More or less my age, he just turned 30 last month.

Pay no attention to such drivel; you are forgetting that critics of that stamp also knock down *your* work.

Trust me, you'll admire the songs. What is more, I'll wager that they will even take your mind off your nephew.

Gladly, I'll leave them with you.

There is no rush, keep them as long as you like.

———

Prospero, Father will be pleased that you like the frame. It was his idea to use black wood and make it very simple.

I don't quite know, only that the shop is in the Graben. My piano teacher took it there.

Are you completely satisfied?

You don't find anything amiss?

Are you absolutely sure?

Even I, who spell like a guttersnipe, was quick to notice: "Jos. Hayden's Birthplace in Rohrau."

Unfortunately my piano teacher wrote it.

It's unfair to judge him by his spelling.

But he is not an ignoramus.

On the contrary he is a very good teacher.

I must object to your calling him that.

Please don't be so angry. In truth it's all *my* fault.

Because I'm the one who wrote the inscription.

I lied a moment ago.

I'm not lying now.

I beg you to believe me.

Very well, I *am* lying. But it's still my fault.

Because Father forbade me to mention the mistake.

He thought that you wouldn't notice it.

For heaven's sake please don't turn against Father too.

I can't take the picture back home until I stop crying.

I should never have disobeyed him. Not only am I now in hot water with Father, but with you and my teacher and the framer and everyone!

If the mistake is corrected, will you change your mind and not demand that my teacher be discharged?

And will I still be welcome here?

Then I'll take it back home and swallow my medicine.

———

Great Maestro, without knowing what Wegeler said in his letter, I can hardly help you frame a reply.

No, I never saw it. Most likely you received it in December before I came back to look after your affairs.

If the letter was here last week it must still be here. Perhaps it's in your portable writing desk.

You will not guess where it was: between the pages of Plutarch.

From what Wegeler says I gather that you planned to send him a portrait of yourself but clean forgot.

There is one in the writing desk.

I'll fetch it as soon as we finish.

VIENNA, FEBRUARY 17, 1827

My worthy old Friend!

It was fortunate that I received from Breuning your second letter at any rate. I am still too weak to reply to it. But you can imagine how welcome and delightful to me are all your remarks. My recovery, if I may call it so, is still very slow. Presumably I must expect a fourth operation, although the doctors have not yet said anything about this. I cultivate patience and think: well, sometimes some good comes from all this evil.—But indeed I was surprised to read in your last letter that you had not yet received anything.

Great Maestro, excuse me but there is someone in the entrance hall.

It's Wolfmayer, he is taking off his things. He says that the snow is now quite deep.

The letter can wait until I come back tomorrow.

If you wish to sit up let me adjust the pillows.

An armchair would surely be more comfortable, not only for your guests but for you, yet a decent one is costly.

I'll send him in to you.

Dear Friend, it has been much too long.

By no means bearing gifts, the wine is solely for medicinal purposes; there is but one small trifle.

Allow me to put it around your shoulders.

camel's hair

Not at all extravagant, it's a perfectly ordinary shawl. Still, I'm glad that I brought it—your hands are cold.

Don't say such things. Admittedly you were heavier when I saw you last, but even so you are far from skin and bones, thank God. We must fatten you up.

No appetite even for fish?

Unfortunately there is no way around that, the fluid has to be tapped.

A fourth operation!

But you mustn't lose heart. Only with patience will you recover and be able to work again.

You still have many works to compose—I trust that you've not forgotten my Requiem.

Come now, I was joking. Even if you fail to write a note of it, I don't expect you to repay the commission.

Doctors are a different matter, naturally.

Supposing that Malfatti refuses to forego his fee, how much is he owed?

And the others?

In short, a goodly sum.

That was smart of you—please disregard the pun. And have you heard from him as yet or from Stumpff?

The Philhar. Soc. will likely stand by its offer; however, it might take a month or more before you hear from them. In the meantime what will you do for funds?

Believe me, I wasn't thinking of the bank shares. Not only do I understand but thoroughly respect your wish not to touch them.

Please calm yourself, anxiety is harmful.

Rest assured that as long as I live you will not want for wine or fuel or candles, nay, for anything; nor will you have to do without your Sali.

I'm sorry it has that appearance; in no sense am I moved by charity. Indeed let me invert what you said earlier: it is I who will never be able to repay you.

For what! Why, for your music.

Please don't be so modest. More than anything that I can think of, your music has transformed my life.

But there *will* be new works—you must not lose hope! As Schubert has it in his Faith in Spring:

The world grows fairer every day,
We cannot know what is still to come,
Unending is the flowering.

It's from a poem by Uhland.

That would make Schubert extremely happy. You can't imagine how he reveres you.

Which of the songs do you most admire?

As soon as the operation is successfully over, I'll ask Hüttenbrenner to bring him by. Meanwhile I beg you to dismiss all thought of privations; your admirers in London, to say nothing of Vienna, will not fail you.

Adieu, dear friend.

———

Great Maestro, if I reacted with surprise perhaps it's because you've decided to dedicate the quartet that you yourself regard as your greatest to a draper.

By no means is it a question of snobbery but of proportion. In recompense for a shawl the reward seems overly generous.

I realize that there is more to the friendship than gift-giving.

Then do let us get on with the letter to Artaria.

On the contrary the mistake is mine. I now see that it's not Artaria; the German publisher Schotts has the C sharp minor quartet, Artaria has the one in B flat.

VIENNA, FEBRUARY 22, 1827

Gentlemen!

I received your last letter through Kreutzer, the Kapellmeister. For the moment I am replying only to the necessary points. The opus (the C sharp minor quartet) which you have is preceded by the one which Matthias Artaria has. Thus you can easily ascertain the number. The dedication is as follows: Dedicated to my friend Johann Nepomuk Wolfmayer.

Now I have a very important request to make—My doctor has prescribed for me some very good old Rhine wine. Even if I were to offer an excessively large sum I could not obtain unadulterated Rhine wine in Vienna. So if I could have a small number of bottles I would show my gratitude. I am inclined to think that something might be arranged for me at the Customs Office so that the cost of the transport would not be too high—As soon as my health permits, you will receive the metronome markings for the Mass as well. But at the moment I am just about to undergo a fourth operation—Hence the sooner I receive this Rhine wine or Moselle wine, the more beneficial it will be to me in my present condition;—and with all my heart I do beg you to do me this kindness for which I shall be gratefully obliged to you.

With kindest regards I remain, Sir, your most devoted

BEETHOVEN

Great Maestro, it's a good sign that you feel well enough to dictate several more. But surely Stumpff will by now have brought your request to the attention of both the Phil. Soc. and your friend Moscheles. As for Sir Smart there is little use in writing him a second letter when you haven't yet received the translation of the first.

Strictly speaking I said that you should expect it by the 20th; unfortunately the 20th fell the day before yesterday.

Your nephew's duties cannot occupy him night and day. Besides, his foremost duty remains to you.

Frankly I find his behavior disgraceful. In all likelihood your brother is right when he says that the boy hasn't time to translate the letter because he is too busy enjoying the winter carnival.

In that case I'll say no more.

I will of course take down the two additional letters if you insist. But I would recommend that you leave the one to Smart in German this time. I would further recommend that we put both aside until we have had a glass of wine and something to eat.

———

Great Maestro, do you mean to say that he doesn't even mention the translation?

What then did he find time to mention?

IGLAU, FEBRUARY 23, 1827

Dear Father,

My heartfelt thanks for the money and the flute score.

The concert was a complete success! I must fall in now for drill.

In the greatest haste, your loving son

KARL

Delinquency puts it mildly, your nephew is utterly irresponsible. Thank goodness I had the sagacity to suggest that the second letter to Smart be left in German.

That is unkind; surely I deserve something more for my pains than the Order of the Jackass, First Class.

It so happens that there are only 340 gulden left in the cashbox.

But you can't economize more than you already do on beef and vegetables without bringing yourself to starvation.

———

Ludwig, as you know, I was opposed to your approaching Smart. Since, however, you did so despite my opinion, I find your nephew's failure to translate the letter inexcusable. Why, even my Gerhard, whose English is negligible, would by now have provided you with a satisfactory translation.

Not only are you about to undergo another operation, but you are in a state of constant anxiety about your debts. Nevertheless you stint yourself to send your nephew money. And how does he requite your kindness? He cannot find the time to translate a two page letter. Clearly the boy is undeserving of your generosity.

Never mind the pocket money, my thoughts are on your will.

Indeed I don't think you should disown him, yet I do think you should sell a bank share.

It's not a matter of the whole inheritance but merely of one share.

I can see that you are adamant.

If you view it as stealing, perhaps you should request his *permission* to sell a share.

Forgive my irony, I did not mean—I am only concerned to make things easier for you, whereas you are only concerned to make things easier for him.

Believe me, I understand how much the bank shares mean to you or, rather, how much *bequeathing them to your nephew* means to you.

Forgive me again. He is, of course, a son to you. Doubtless I would do the same for Gerhard.

May God preserve you, Ludwig.

———

Prospero, I heard today that the bedbugs are tormenting you and wake you constantly.

You need to sleep. I'll get something to drive them away. Meanwhile when you see one, stick it with a needle; you'll soon get rid of them.

Then let us change the subject. How was your dinner today?

But the doctor says that you need to eat meat.

In that case I suspect that the ham was not good to begin with. When you buy so little they just don't care and throw in any old thing.

That's happened to Mother many times, that something entirely different from what she ordered is brought to the table.

Schindler let drop that he doesn't really like ham and noodles. At least you may be sure he always likes the wine.

Don't be angry about it. If you were not so good-natured, you would ask him to pay for his board.

I have to leave now, I'm going to theater at 7:30.

Goodness! I almost forgot. Father and Mother and I fervently hope that tomorrow's operation will light the way to full recovery and also an end to your financial worries.

Father will be surprised to hear that.

He really doubted that the translation would arrive before the operation, if ever. I'll tell him.

———

Esteemed Patient, I am pleased to say that the surgery is successfully over; relief will soon be evident.

I grant you that the tappings are no more than palliative.

Nevertheless we have come to the end of February; soon winter's adverse effects upon your dropsy will subside. With spring you will feel revitalized.

I entreat you not to lose heart.

Rest assured that you will work again.

Neither you nor your work is finished. Need I remind you that your two grand pianos are but a step away? With the help of your physician you will soon return to them.

Why do you smile?

Who knows, you may yet regard me as wonderful.

Ah! now I recognize the words. They are from Handel's *Messiah*, albeit somewhat muddled.

Perhaps you are right, perhaps only the Physician whose name is Wonderful can help you now. If so, that is the principal reason not to abandon hope—nil desperandum

Well and good. Now Councilor Breuning wishes to have a word with you.

Ludwig, once more you have taught us all the lesson of the Stoics; I am humbled by your patience.

You must cheer up, dejection prevents your getting better.

Before we leave, Gerhard has a message for you from Wolfmayer.

Prospero, he went away as soon as it was over but sent you his fondest regards.

Wolfmayer loves you very much; before leaving there were tears in his eyes and he said, "Oh, the great man. Ach! the pity of it."

He asked if you still have wine.

Even better, he said that as soon as you feel well enough, he'll bring Schubert to you.

May I be present when he does?

I would like to take Schubert's coat for him.

Then I'll pray that he visits midday, when I come from school.

———

Great Maestro, Schubert and Hüttenbrenner are here.

But Wolfmayer never planned to accompany them; they came with me.

In that case Gerhard garbled the message.

Usually Hütten. acts as Schubert's intermediary: he does much, if not most, of the talking.

Of course you may see Schubert alone; I'll send him in to you.

———

Revered Maestro, it's not the cat that has my tongue.

If I must confess, it's you.

Please don't misunderstand me, I really—it's simply that—in truth I am by nature shy.

It is indeed a fine lithograph.

I am hard put to answer.

Naturally, I should have guessed since Haydn was your teacher.

Mine? I would have to say, I mean, my debt to you—it's *you* whom I would emulate.

You are much too generous. Frankly I now consider many of my earlier songs long-winded.

I prefer more recent ones; they are more concise.

For example I might cite "The Young Nun." Perhaps you had time to glance at it?

If I'm blushing, it's because—Again you are too generous.

You didn't find the ringing of the convent bell overdone?

Thank you, that makes me breathe easier.

"The Almighty" was written some six months later.

Dear me, but I know of no way to govern blushing.

True enough. However, I disagree with you about the final line; it is never too late to hope for grace and mercy—Sometimes the Almighty

No, no, I—no one said a word, neither Schindler nor Wolfmayer said a word about dying. In regard to your premonition, three years ago I too believed that I was at death's door. Yet as you see . . .

I realize that you are 56 and I have just turned 30, that your cheeks are sunken and mine are fat—Would to God I could give you my unneeded fat!

My apologies, tears are even more embarrassing than blushes.

If only widows are meant to cry, my tears are inappropriate. Still, it's clear to me that if you die, I shall feel—well, if not, strictly speaking, widowed—orphaned.

I had better leave now, lest I baptize you with tears. Thank you for permitting me to visit.

Shall I send in Hüttenbrenner?

I'll tell him you are tired but extend your warmest greetings.

May God keep you, Maestro.

———

Brother, when I saw our sister-in-law yesterday I mentioned your fourth operation.

Come now, it's hardly a secret—all Vienna knows how gravely ill you are.

Frankly I think it behooves you to invite her here.

Why do you look for ulterior motives where none exist?

Seeing that her son is your sole heir, her hands are more or less *already* on the bank shares.

As I told you in January, in the event of his death, God forbid, the one way to keep her from acquiring the capital would be to hold it in trust—In that case you could arrange for Karl to receive the interest for the rest of his life; after his death it would pass to his *legitimate offspring*.

Codicils are useless—Bach will simply have to draw up a new will.

Don't upset yourself, there is still time to weigh the matter—But apropos of the bank shares, I've been thinking that

Clearly the only thing that comes from Schindler's mouth is shit—Snooping indeed! On the contrary I've been searching for them openly—And a good thing, too. Just imagine what a pickle we'd be in if you gave up the ghost and no one knew where the bank shares were hidden.

And who, if I may ask, might that be?

Come now, what is the good of "someone who knows," if no one knows who that someone is?

I'm in no mood for guessing games, nor have I time for such nonsense. I'll look in on you tomorrow.

―――――

Great Maestro, how contrary of you to misplace your spectacles on the day that a letter finally arrives from your nephew.

Have you no idea when you last wore them?

If you were searching for Sir Smart's address, then they must be in the next room.

Just where you left them: on the desk with the letters.

But surely I handed you your nephew's letter when I went in search of the spectacles.

My mistake, here it is.

My dear Father,

I have just received the boots you sent me and thank you very much for them. You will have received the translation of the letter to Smart; I have no doubt that it will bring the desired result.

Just today a cadet, who had been in Vienna on a furlough, returned to his battalion, and he reports having heard that you were saved by some sort of sherbert and are feeling much better. I hope that the latter is true whatever the means may have been. There is little new to tell about myself. The service goes as usual, the only difference being that the weather is much milder which makes guard duty more agreeable.

Write me very soon about the state of your health; also please give my warm regards to the Councilor. I kiss you.

Great Maestro, what has he done now to cause you such a burst of tears?

Forgive me, I assumed that you had finished; by all means do read the postscript.

Your loving son
KARL

P.S. Please stamp your letters because I have to pay a lot of postage here for which I hardly have enough in my account.

Great Maestro, rest assured that henceforth I'll stamp them here.

Now, if you have fully digested his letter, it's time for your frozen punch. And I'll join you, if I may, with a nice glass of red.

By no means does my "burning thirst" preclude my taking down a letter to Sir Smart. Let us set to work.

VIENNA, MARCH 6, 1827

Sir!

No doubt, Sir, you have already received through Moscheles my letter of February 22nd. Nevertheless since I happen to have found your address among my papers, I do not hesitate to write to you direct and to urge most insistently that you fulfill my request.

Unfortunately as yet I cannot foresee the end of my dreadful illness. On the contrary, my sufferings and my anxieties coupled with them have only increased—On February 27th I was operated on for the fourth time; and perhaps Fate may decide that I must expect this for a fifth time or even more often. If this is going to continue, my illness will certainly persist until the middle of the summer. And if so, what is to become of me? What am I to live on until I have recovered my lost strength and can again earn my living by means of my pen?—But I must be brief and not trouble you, Sir, with fresh complaints. I merely refer to my letter of February 22nd and beg you to exert all your influence to induce the Philharmonic Society to carry out now their former decision to give a concert for my benefit—My strength is not equal to saying anything more on this subject. Moreover I am too deeply convinced of your noble and friendly treatment of me to fear that I shall be misunderstood.

Accept the assurance of my highest esteem and be convinced that, while anxiously awaiting an early reply,

I shall ever remain, Sir, your most devoted

LUDWIG VAN BEETHOVEN

Great Maestro, with your permission I shall now fetch the refreshments.

———

Prospero, Mother promises to have the roast squabs for you on Sunday. Meanwhile she hopes that these stewed apricots are to your liking.

Did you enjoy Hummel's visit yesterday?

Naturally it tired you; Father told me that you got up and sat in a chair the whole time.

I'm sorry to have missed him; first it was Schubert and now Hummel.

I find his music a bit shallow.

In my opinion there is no contest, Schubert wins hands down.

I must leave. But Father wishes to have a word with you before going back to the War Department.

In that case I'll tell him to come now.

Ludwig, this morning the Lieutenant Field-Marshal sent word that he wished to see me this afternoon. When I questioned his adjutant about the object of the meeting, the man would only say that it pertained to your nephew.

I have no idea. Was there any mention of trouble in his recent letter?

It's useless to speculate on the matter until we learn more.

Do try not to be too anxious; I'll give you a full report this evening.

Ludwig, it seems that von Stutterheim has heard some gossip about your nephew's suicide attempt.

He did not mention the source, nor did I inquire.

I held fast to what I said last summer: that he was recuperating from a hernia operation.

Although I did not deny the suicide attempt, I did my best to play it down, dismissing the incident as but another example of a lovelorn youth imitating Werther.

I have no idea whether he believed me or, indeed, whether he plans to take further steps.

He might do one of several things—But it's useless to anticipate his action.

"Influence him" in what way?

I would say that von Stutterheim, not unlike many others, has an amateur's love of music.

No doubt he would be greatly flattered, nay more, thunderstruck!

Are you sure you wish to make such a princely gesture?

Well and good, but do not act in haste; I urge you to sleep on it.

———

Great Maestro, I sincerely hope that your change of heart has nothing to do with my calling Wolfmayer a draper.

I know better than to make the same mistake twice; the letter will of course go to Schotts.

VIENNA, MARCH 10, 1827

Gentlemen!

According to my letter the quartet was to be dedicated to someone whose name I had already sent you. But something has happened which has decided me to make an alteration in this respect. The quartet must now be dedicated to the Lieutenant Field-Marshal Baron von Stutterheim to whom I am indebted for many kindnesses. If you have perhaps already engraved the first dedication, I beg you for Heaven's sake to alter it, and I will gladly compensate you for the expense of doing so. Do not treat my remarks as empty promises. Indeed this matter is of such importance to me that I will gladly and readily reimburse you to any extent whatever.

I enclose the title.

As for the parcel to my friend, the Royal Prussian Regierungsrat von Wegeler at Coblenz, I am delighted to be able to relieve you entirely of this commission. For an opportunity has been found to dispatch everything to him direct.

My health, which will not be restored for a very long time, requires that you should send me the wines I asked you for. They will certainly bring me refreshment, invigoration and good health.

I remain, Sir, with most sincere regards, your most devoted

LUDWIG VAN BEETHOVEN

Great Maestro, in order to make amends you might consider dedicating the quartet in F to Wolfmayer.

I believe that Schlesinger owns it.

I still have time to take it down, unless you are too tired.

Then by all means rest, there is no pressing urgency to write the letter today.

———

Dear Tone Poet,
    Look for me at about three o'clock this afternoon.

Your faithful

MALFATTI

———

Great Maestro, even though he hasn't been here all week, rest assured that Malfatti is fully aware of your suffering.

I very much doubt that he has hit upon a new prescription. On the other hand, perhaps he has, I mean, hit upon something that may at least alleviate these terrible atacks of pain.

With Malfatti there is always the possibility of miracles.

Since it is now 2:45 you will soon have your answer.

———

Beethoven, I am deeply sorry to find you in this grievous state.

I have in fact brought you something which, though in no wise a new prescription, will surely ease your suffering.

Gumpoldskirchner, it's the best wine available for the frozen punch.

You overstate my generosity, I have brought but two bottles.

I do indeed remember my original prescription; unfortunately it is impossible to obtain a genuine Moselle in Vienna.

I hope you will enjoy it. To that end I am setting aside all restrictions on the quantity: from now on you may have more than one glass a day.

Or even three if you like, as long as you do not overdo it. You yourself must be the judge of that.

Believe me when I say that they are being set aside not because you are dying but because you are suffering. As your doctor, let alone your friend, I will not have you languish in pain.

As soon as you like. You may have a glass forthwith.

I have already rung for her.

Well then, when she comes I will tell her that Schindler is not to touch the Gumpoldskirchner.

———

Brother, I am in fact in pleasurable suspension—not unlike yourself.

In my case it has nothing to do with Gumpoldskirchner.

Presumably you mean to tell me now where the bank shares are hidden.

Then why did you send for me?

Well, that at least is something.

Relations between you and our sister-in-law are too delicate for such offhand behavior—you would do better to write her a note.

Because it's better form.

Clearly you are too inebriated for me to argue the point—I'll transmit the invitation verbally.

———

Great Maestro, since we still have time let us finish the letter to Moscheles.

You had just expressed your conviction that with the help of Smart and Stumpff etc. the Phil. Soc. would come to your aid.

On February 27th I underwent a fourth operation; and already there are visible signs again that I must soon undergo a fifth. What is to be the end of it all? And what is to become of me, if my illness persists for some time?—Truly my lot is a very hard one! However, I am resigned to accept whatever Fate may bring; and I only continue to pray that God in His divine wisdom may so order events that as long as I have to endure this living death, I may be protected from want. This would give me sufficient strength to bear my lot, however difficult and terrible it may prove to be, with a feeling of submission to the will of the Almighty.

So, my dear Moscheles, I again ask you to deal with this matter which concerns me; and I remain with my most cordial regards ever your friend

L. V. BEETHOVEN

P.S. Hummel is here and has already visited me a few times.

Great Maestro, may I enclose a brief note with the letter?

Nothing more than my greetings.

My dear Moscheles,

Hummel and his wife came here hurriedly in order to see Beethoven while he is still alive, for it is reported in Germany that he is on his deathbed. It was a most touching sight last Thursday to witness the reunion of these two old friends.

In haste, yours
SCHINDLER

———

Great Maestro, good news! Mr. Rau of the banking house of Eskeles is here.

He is the major-domo of Baron Eskeles. Indeed, was it not the Baron who originally advised you to purchase the bank shares?

The Almighty works in mysterious ways. Rau, you see, is also a friend of Moscheles, to say nothing of mine; thus I suspect that his visit relates in some way to the Phil. Soc.

I'll show him in.

———

Venerated Composer, I am truly sorry to find you in such poor health.

And to think that I, who live in Vienna, knew nothing of your illness nor of your privation, whereas Mr. Moscheles, who lives in London, knew everything.

His letter just arrived this morning. The moment I finished perusing it, I left the bank and came here straightway.

But there was also mention of a letter to you. Have you not received it?

It will likely be delivered tomorrow.

In short, at a meeting held on February 28th the directors of the Philharmonic Society resolved to send you, through the good offices of Mr. Moscheles, a long overdue benefaction. You are to receive as a loan the sum of 100 pounds sterling (1000 gulden) to provide whatever necessities and comforts you may find wanting.

Shall I step out for a moment?

Rest assured that I am not embarrassed; however, I do not wish to intrude.

Words are unnecessary, your tears acknowledge all.

Excuse me but I do not follow you. What is for your nephew?

I asked only because you mentioned him.

Then let us continue. When I write to Mr. Moscheles I will certainly relate your deep-felt expressions of gratitude. As for the money, you will have it first thing in the morning.

Well and good. On the other hand you might prefer to take only half of it tomorrow and leave the rest with the Baron. It is after all quite a large sum to have lying about the apartment.

If 500 will not suffice, by all means take the 1000; the money is yours to do with as you please. I can only hope that it will bring you swift relief or, better still, an unforseen recovery.

One can never tell—Dr. Malfatti is a very clever physician.

I shall return in the morning. Meanwhile may heaven be with you.

———

Venerated Composer, good morning. Clearly your housekeeper is extremely upset.

Did it burst while you were sleeping?

Has Dr. Malfatti been informed?

Do you not think he ought to be?

After such a mishap, it is a wonder to find you in such good cheer.

Why do you say thanks to *me*?

Ah, but of course! Then do let us proceed. On behalf of Mr. Moscheles and the Philharmonic Society of London, it gives me great satisfaction to present you with this timely relief.

Further, I must trouble you for your signature on this receipt.

Thank you kindly, but I suspect that the messenger of the gods was a good deal more fleet than I am.

Before departing I urge you, if only for my own peace of mind, to let me apprise Dr. Malfatti of what has happened.

Believe me, it is no trouble; I shall take a cab there and back.

That is most kind of you; however, you are not to spend the money on anyone but yourself. What is more, you may be sure that the Baron will reimburse me for the cab.

———

Venerated Composer, I am delighted to report that when I told Dr. Malfatti what had happened, he welcomed the news.

Evidently it spares you for the present the necessity of having another operation. What is more, he said that he will now contrive to keep the wound open so that the fluid can drain freely.

He surmises that the rupture was brought on by your sense of financial relief.

Believe me, it was no trouble. Now, however, I must return to the bank.

Please do not mention it; I am deeply honored to have been of service to you.

———

Brother, it goes without saying that I'm pleased as punch to hear of your good fortune; yet to hear of it from a virtual stranger while finishing off a piece of business, however profitable, is downright embarrassing.

May I know how much you received?

A rather tidy sum, to say the least.

Doctors' fees aside, on what do you plan to spend it?

But since you have difficulty chewing beef it's idle to speak of it. You'll just have to settle for a nice piece of fish.

I saw some pike-perch in the market yesterday—they looked delicious; so, too, did the salmon trout.

No, but I did spot a string of plump quail.

Edibles aside, on what else do you plan to spend the funds?

I understand—for a rainy day, so to speak.

Well, I needn't tell you how much good it does my heart to see you this happy—Perhaps you are more inclined now to reveal the whereabouts of the bank shares.

By God, I'm sick of hearing that! With your newly acquired wealth you ought to buy a parrot and have it trained to say, "There is one who knows." Adieu!

———

Great Maestro, I know without asking that Rau has been here.

Because I haven't seen you so care-free since Malfatti first prescribed the frozen punch. Besides, I encountered your brother in the entrance hall.

Needless to say he is searching for the bank shares.

Pay no attention. You may not be able to chew beefsteak but you surely can manage ragout, not to mention ox-tongue and sweet-breads and liver, etc.

If they were in the market yesterday, they will likely be found there tomorrow. What could be more appetizing than a couple of quail for Sunday dinner.

In that case I'll also tell her to keep an eye out for pike-perch and salmon trout. And while we are on the subject let us not forget wine.

It occurs to me that you might want to replenish your store of Gumpoldskirchner.

I beg your pardon but I never even tasted it. I speak of it now simply because you were so enamored of the bottles Malfatti brought. Besides, it would go especially well with the fish.

But I'm content with whatever you serve me.

All joking aside, the most ordinary table wine

Believe me, I would be more than

Do let us drop the subject.—When Schubert was here, and afterwards Hummel, you were greatly embarrassed, and rightly so, by the condition of your easy chair. Frankly, this one is ready for the junk heap.

Hardly an amenity, in my opinion a new one is a necessity. In fact it's just the sort of comfort that the Phil. Soc. had in mind for you.

By all means have leather. Seeing that you have to sit in it every day while the girl makes up the bed, you should have whatever you fancy. I'll see what is offered in the flea market.

The money is indeed a godsend, for which Moscheles is mostly to be thanked.

Unfortunately I cannot take down the letter now; I have a performance this afternoon. I'll do so tomorrow.

Drinking songs! Rest assured that there are none on the program. But speaking of drinking, may I ask how many glasses of punch you have had?

In my view that is one too many.

———

VIENNA, MARCH 18, 1827

My dear, kind Moscheles!

I cannot put into words the emotion with which I read your letter of March 1st. The Philharmonic Society's generosity in almost anticipating my appeal has touched my innermost soul.—I request you, therefore, dear Moscheles, to be the spokesman through whom I send to the Philharmonic Society my warmest and most heartfelt thanks for their special sympathy and support.

I found myself obliged to draw immediately the whole sum of 1000 gulden, for I just happened to be in the unpleasant position of having to borrow money; and this would have caused me fresh embarrassment.

In regard to the concert which the Philharmonic Society has decided to give for my benefit, I do beg the Society not to give up this noble plan but to deduct from the proceeds of this concert the 1000 gulden which they have already advanced me. And if the Society will be so kind as to let me have the remainder, I will undertake to return to the Society my warmest thanks by engaging to compose for it either a new symphony, sketches for which are already in my desk, or a new overture, or something else which the Society might like to have.

May heaven but restore my health very soon and I shall prove to those magnanimous Englishmen how greatly I appreciate their sympathy for me in my sad fate.

But *your* noble behavior I shall never forget; and I will shortly proceed to express my thanks particularly to Sir Smart and Mr. Stumpff.

I wish you all happiness! With the most friendly sentiments I remain your friend who highly esteems you

LUDWIG VAN BEETHOVEN

My heartfelt greetings to your wife.

I am indebted to the Philharmonic Society and yourself for a new friend, namely, Mr. Rau. Please let the Philharmonic Society have the metronome tempi for the symphony. I send you the markings herewith.

Great Maestro, rest assured that I will copy them with care.

———

Brother, on my way in I crossed paths with Wawruch; he said you have but little strength today.

I'm sorry to hear that, and sorry, too, for losing my temper with you yesterday—my apologies.

Come now, do you imagine that I'm planning to steal the bank shares?

Then why do you play this childish game with me?

Well and good, but for Karl's sake—or, better still, simply to facilitate the terms of your will, it would be useful to know where they are hidden.

At least tell me the name—merely that—of this all-knowing one.

I took a turn about the room.

to collect myself

Ludwig, it falls to me—I'm really at a loss to find a way—nay, there is no artful way to tell you the unvarnished truth. Wawruch—Malfatti too—both have given up hope.

I'm surprised myself by my tears—You take it better than I do.

According to Wawruch the end cannot be far off. When we met just now he asked me—you'll remember that he studied for the priesthood before he took up medicine. Hence he asked me if I thought you would be willing to receive the Holy Sacrament.

I told him that even though you are somewhat careless about attending church, in all likelihood you are more religious than he is—witness your grand solemn Mass.

Of course I didn't put it in those words. Still, I happen to agree with him in regard to Extreme Unction.

Brother, I cannot urge you strongly enough to make your peace with God.

By no means at this moment—at the appropriate time, naturally.

Again I'm surprised—I didn't expect you to agree with such alacrity—That leaves unsettled only the disposition of your estate.

As for our sister-in-law, I made a mistake—I should have stayed out of it.

I did indeed extend the invitation—Added to that, I tugged at her heartstrings, but to no avail—She doesn't wish to see you.

She gave no reason, nor did I press her for one.

Not a word was said about your legal battle.

Even though it ended seven years ago, her wounds may not as yet have healed.

It goes without saying that you were wounded too.

Perhaps she is less forgiving than you are.

Frankly I don't know what would sway her. Unless—yes! You might frame the request as a deathbed wish.

No need to wait for Schindler; surely I can pen it just as well as Mr. Shitting—better! I'll wager.

My dear Sister-in-law,

Now that the doctors have given up hope, the possibility that we might never again see each other does not sit well with me. To forestall that event I entreat you to come to Schwarzpanier House tomorrow morning at about ten o'clock. Do find it in your heart to grant me this final wish.

In haste, your devoted brother-in-law

LUDWIG

———

Ludwig, clearly you are not ready for me; you should have said 10:30.

She went to fetch a glass of frozen punch.

Yes, she apologized and blamed the disorder on the delivery of a chair.

The one I'm sitting in?

Have you yourself not sat in it?

It's perfectly comfortable.

If I averted my eyes—Well, you'll have to excuse me but nothing prepared me for how thin you are.—Here is the punch.

Let me help you, it's dribbling all over your night shirt.

Whether or not you feel like a baby, rest assured that you don't resemble one.—Besides, mothers don't feed babies punch.

It's not a bib but my handkerchief; she failed to bring you a napkin.

It's perfumed because—Who knows? Because I like perfume—Do stop interrupting.

No more—it's finished, I set the glass aside.

gardenia

I'm glad the scent pleases you—you who are so unaccustomed to women's things, to women at all.

Certainly you may hold the handkerchief for a moment—providing that it doesn't turn you into Othello.

If I had a kronen for every time you called me a whore—But never mind, that isn't why you sent for me. Well now, why did you?

I was taught not to answer a question by asking one.

For my part I came here—Duty! pure and simple, I considered it my duty to respect your wishes. Needless to say that you are still the head of the family. But to come back to you, why did

Another? Surely it's forbidden to have more than one glass.

I don't care what the doctor says—all those ices cannot be good for your stomach.

No need to make a fuss, I'll go and fetch another.

Don't speak with your mouth full—I cannot understand a word you say.

Don't gulp so. I'll still be here when it's finished.

If you expect me to feed you, I'll thank you to do it at my pace.

There now, so much for the second serving.

Indeed I am surprised; I was sure that your eyes were bigger than your stomach. Still, it's a good sign—at least you haven't lost your appetite completely.

Before you go on, do answer my question—Why in fact did you send for me?

Don't be bashful—out with it.

I know that Karl is your sole heir, if that is your meaning.

Naturally, never for a moment did I assume that you wished to harm *him*; throughout the whole ordeal I realized that your malevolence was aimed at *me*.

Come now, was it not malevolent to allege in a court of law that I had poisoned your brother!

That may be, but you believed it at the time. You also believed that I tried to poison my son. And added to that, you asserted that I was depraved, plague-ridden and pestilential—in short, that I was *the scum of the earth*!

The words are yours, *all of them*, to say nothing of the aforementioned whore—or, as you minced it in your mendacious Appeal, I was unfit to be a mother because I was "a woman of easy virtue."

If my councilor asserted that you were unfit to be a father—well, at least his object was not to defame you; he did so for practical reasons.

Not only your deafness, but your utter lack of experience; after all, you hadn't the slightest idea of how to care for a child. Why, the first time Karl ran away from you his hands and feet were frostbitten, his linen hadn't been changed in a week.

Let's not rehearse the charges; admittedly there were faults on both sides. Still, I would have suffered all in silence, had you but permitted me to spend some time with him.

Once a month is hardly adequate for a mother, let alone a child.—You said in your note that the prospect of never seeing me again did not sit well with you. Imagine how it sits with a mother.

Rubbish! On one occasion you made certain that I was barred from seeing him for *eight months*. You can't possibly imagine the grievousness, nay, cruelty of such a prohibition.

I don't mean you alone, no man can imagine it—least of all a woman-hater like yourself.

I beg your pardon but you *are* a woman-hater. In your eyes a woman is either a madonna or a whore who will give you the clap.

Spare me! When it comes to women your ignorance, indeed the ignorance of all the Beethoven men, is dumfounding—Oh, how I wish your brother had heeded your advice not to marry me! But by then, of course, the whore was carrying his child.

If I took a lover during his final months, your brother brought it on himself—his brutality had long since finished off fidelity.

Come now, surely you remember how vicious he could be; surely you haven't forgotten, say, the time he drove a knife through the back of my hand.

My object was to show you the scar, not—What prompted you to kiss my hand?

That was kind of you, but I'm no longer the least bit aware of the scar.

You need hardly apologize for kissing my hand, nor for your tears.

At last!

Oh Ludwig, thank you, thank you—I never expected to hear those words pass your lips.

I realize, naturally, how difficult it was to speak them—Well, at least I understand now why you sent for me.

If only you had asked my forgiveness seven years ago—not even my forgiveness, if only you had found a way, I mean had made the smallest gesture—But no matter, it's water under the bridge.

A gesture of kindness, simply that—if instead of enmity you had found a way to show your *heart*

Were it in my power, I would gladly forgive you, but only God can forgive our trespasses.

Which of the Gospels?

To be sure, I had forgotten.

No, no, what it says more or less is this: if you don't forgive others and do so from the heart, you yourself won't be forgiven by God.

Then let me do so now—I forgive you, Ludwig—for everything—I forgive you.

Rest assured that it comes from my heart.

There now, that's enough, you have cried enough for one day—indeed we both have. Do let me dry your tears.

I can't imagine what we would have done without my handker-chief.

Drying your tears is hardly an act of charity.

In what way a turnabout?

Ludwig, the dying woman that you succored was your mother.

But I am Johanna, your sister-in-law.

Listen to me, Ludwig, *I am not your mother.*

Surely you mean Karl

Don't be preposterous—I most certainly

Childbearing may be holy but

Let me assure you

In neither this nor any other bed did I give birth to you!

Ludwig, look at me—take a hard look

There now, don't you see—I am no one but your

Nimbus—what are you saying?

Nonsense! there is no such thing—the curtains are drawn. That may be but there is no light. It is just your fancy. Goddess?

Clearly the punch

Of course I recognize the words, but why

Why are you singing Ode to Joy?

You are utterly confused—the Daughter of Elysium is Mother Nature—I am quite mortal.

Believe me, I am merely mortal.

Well then, if it makes you happy—yes! I am indeed the Daughter of Elysium.

Yes indeed I have descended.

I was not speaking but singing—I, too, am singing!

Joy! Joy!
Praise to joy the God descended—

Now, now, no more for today—you will strain yourself. But I am not
ill, whereas you

Very well, but only one more time.

Joy! Joy!
Praise to joy the God descended—

Now that's enough.

No! Enough is enough—now you must rest!

By all means keep the handkerchief, providing that you rest.

Here's a joyous kiss for all!

May God preserve you, Ludwig.

————

Great Maestro, since Dr. Bach is still indisposed, Councilor Breuning has drafted the codicil.

My nephew Karl shall be my sole legatee, but the capital of my
estate shall fall to his legitimate or testamentary heirs.
                                          Vienna, March 23, 1827
                              LUDWIG VAN BEETHOVEN

Great Maestro, it is intentionally brief so that the transcription will
not overtax you.

The copy must be in your own hand.

I find nothing to question about legitimate.

With what word would you replace it?

Presumably Breuning is now at the War Department; he will come here midday to witness the signing.

Your brother is already here.

It goes without saying what he is up to.

I'll fetch him.

———

Brother, clearly Breuning's object is to keep Johanna from acquiring the capital—I must say that for once I agree with His Highness.

But that happens to be *your object* too—legitimate simply connotes your own wishes.

Have you some other word in mind?

To substitute for legitimate?

If none has yet occurred to you, none most likely will—We had better let it stand. Don't you agree?

I'm waiting to hear that you agree.

Why, to sign the codicil as it's written.

D'accord! Now we have only to wait for His Highness—By the by, am I not right in assuming that he is *the all-knowing one*?

Breuning

A simple yes or no will suffice.

Stubborn to the last!

———

Ludwig, have you read the codicil?

Are you in agreement with what is written there?

Have you the strength to copy it?

Dearest friend, forever dauntless! But take your time, there is no hurry.

Do not concern yourself, I shall ink the pen.

    My nephew Karl shall be my sole legatee but the capital of my state shall fall to his natural or testamentary heirs.

Vienna, March 23, 1827

LUWIG VAN BEETHOEN

Ludwig, unfortunately there is a mistake.

For "legitimate" you have written "natural."

On no account do they mean the same thing. If you allow "natural" to stand, your sister-in-law

You need only write

I am not asking you to write more words but only

Kindly *restore legitimate*

If you cannot, you cannot—So be it then.

———

Brother, presumably you haven't forgotten your willingness to receive the Holy Sacrament.

What is the matter—don't you recognize me?

But only yesterday you knew me—I am your brother, Nikolaus Johann.

You sometimes called me Cain.

Be so good as to look again!

One moment please—Johanna wishes to have a word with you.

Ludwig, do you remember these lines?

> Above the star-filled heavens
> A loving Father surely dwells.

Yes exactly, from Ode to Joy! Have you forgotten what follows?

> Dost thou sense thy Maker near?
> Above the star-filled heavens seek Him!

Granted He has always been near—still, it behooves you

Ludwig, Dr. Wawruch urges us to send for the parish priest.

I'll let him speak for himself.

Esteemed Patient, it falls to me to repeat once more and, I may say, for the last time the words of the great Hippocrates: ars longa, vita brevis. Since, however, your art is eternal, it is now incumbent upon you to attend to your eternal soul.

In the name of those assembled here, nay, of those everywhere who revere your music, I entreat you to receive the Holy Sacrament.

Added to that, it will show the whole world that Beethoven is a true Christian.

God be thanked, I will send for the priest.

———

Great Maestro, do not spend yourself in speech. The priest departed long since; you are now truly reconciled with Heaven.

In spite of untold interruptions the letter to Moscheles is indeed finished. I myself have been trying to write him, but to no avail. Nevertheless, you may rest assured that both letters will be posted this afternoon, visitors permitting, or tomorrow at the latest.

———

VIENNA, MARCH 24, 1827

My dear Moscheles,

When you read these lines our friend will no longer be among the living. His death is fast approaching, and all of us have but one wish: to see him released from his terrible suffering. There is nothing else left to hope for. For a week he has lain as though half dead, but has mustered his remaining strength now and then to put a question or to ask for something. His condition is appalling, indeed exactly like the Duke of York's, about which we read recently. He is in a constant state of dull brooding; his head hangs down onto his chest and he stares at one spot for hours at a time. Seldom does he recognize even his closest acquaintances save when he is told who they are. In short, it is dreadful to see. This state of affairs can last but a few days more, for all bodily functions have ceased since yesterday. So, God willing, he shall soon be released, and us with him. People have begun to come in droves to have a last look, although no one is admitted excepting those brazen enough to torment a dying man in his final hours.

His letter to you, which except for a handful of words at the beginning he dictated verbatim, will probably be his last; on the other hand today he whispered to me albeit brokenly: "Smart—Stumpff—write them!" If he can still write as much as his name, I will make sure that it is done.—He knows the end is near, for yesterday he said to me and Councilor v. Breuning: "Plaudite, amici, comoedia finita est!" Also we were fortunate enough yesterday to put his will in order, even though there is nothing here but a few old pieces of funiture and

———

MARCH 26, 1827

Dearest Karli,

Your uncle died this afternoon. If possible, please come at once.

Your loving mother

6

DEAREST KARLI,

At three o'clock when the coffin was closed and carried down-stairs and there was still no sign of you, I assumed that your captain had refused to grant you a furlough; it did not occur to me that snow had delayed the coach—here Monday's snow had completely melted making way for a lovely spring day. As soon as your Aunt Therese saw the throng assembled outside, she was prompted to fancy what certain busybodies, not unlike herself, to be sure, would make of your absence and Amalie's. Imagine! Well, I told her plainly that you as a Beethoven, let alone your uncle's sole heir, were hardly to be lumped together with her daughter. (Had she had the wit to speak of my Ludovica instead of you, she would have made her point, but reasoning has never been Fat Stuff's strong suit.) In any case it was a pity that you arrived too late to attend the funeral and, still worse, that you had to turn right around and take the night coach back. It would have been no skin off your captain's nose had he permitted you to stay the night. Hail Caesar!

This week's events swirl in my mind like wind-blown snow; so, you see, we both have had to brave a snowstorm. Nevertheless I will do my best to sort them out, not only for your sake but mine.—Not long after your Uncle received the Holy Sacrament he lapsed into a coma. For those of us present at the time—in addition to myself there were your Uncle Johann and Aunt Therese, Schindler, Sali, Breuning and, needless to say, that irritating son of his; however bright and well-mannered the boy may be, he is utterly spoiled. But

Gerhard aside, not one of those assembled on Monday afternoon expected your Uncle to survive the night. Well, we could not have been more mistaken. The following morning found him still alive—unconscious, to be sure, and in the throes of the death rattle, but all the same alive. (To give you some idea of how noisy his breathing was, it assaulted one's ears as far away as the coat rack in the entrance hall.) Indeed it struck me as ironical that a composer who created such sublime music in life, should in death create such pig-like noises. All in all the death rattle lasted two days. Just imagine! a man who, as I mentioned in my last letter, had scarcely strength enough to hold the pen with which he copied the codicil, managed nonetheless to hold death at bay for two whole days! But to return to the living, some among those keeping vigil began to grow unnerved—Schindler for one (he is such an old maid), so too your Uncle Johann, albeit with your uncle one never quite knows what is genuine and what is for show; yet worst of all was Breuning who behaved throughout like an overbred bitch. (Considering not only his pallor but the fire in his eyes, I suspect that he himself is not long for this world.)

Well, by Monday afternoon our number had increased. In addition to those already mentioned, a friend of Franz Schubert's, an exceptionally handsome young man named Hüttenbrenner was there, as well as a friend of his, an artist who had come to sketch "the dying composer." Although your Uncle Johann found the artist's presence unobjectionable, nay more, desirable for posterity's sake, it deeply affronted Breuning who had words with the man and threw him out. Soon thereafter Breuning and Schindler took up the question of where to bury your Uncle.

Oddly it was Gerhard, forever on the lookout to please his father, who suggested that Uncle Ludwig be buried at Währing. It so happens that Währing is where Breuning's first wife ("Father's Julie, who died at nineteen," Gerhard informed me) is buried, and where the Councilor himself plans to be laid to rest. At that moment I wondered what the present Mrs. Breuning who, I need hardly remind you, is the mother of his children, makes of her husband's design, but never mind! Gerhard's suggestion pleased his father, naturally; thus Breuning and Schindler set out for Währing in search of a suitable burial plot. (In my opinion they would have seized upon any excuse to flee the death-chamber.) Now it was your Uncle Johann's turn to be affronted. How dared Breuning take the matter on himself! he had no right to select a plot without consulting the composer's brother! etc. Whereupon he, too, set out for Währing. Well, that left only three of us in the death chamber—Hüttenbrenner, Gerhard and myself.

Late in the afternoon—it must have been about 5 o'clock—the room grew suddenly dark. From the windows I saw masses of black clouds gathering or, rather, converging as if by prearrangement—for that is how it seemed—on Schwarzpanier House. Presently the most violent storm broke right overhead; not only was there thunder and lightning, but howling wind and snow, to say nothing of hailstones the size of grapes! Indeed one did not know what to make of it, which month we were in, whether in July or December. In the middle of everything, as though for comical relief, Gerhard was summoned home for his piano lesson. Then all at once a flash of lightning filled the room with glaring light. This was accompanied by a loud thunderclap, so loud in fact—You know the saying that something is loud enough to wake the dead; well, that is more or less what happened! I don't mean that your Uncle did in truth hear the thunderclap, but only that it *seemed so* to us who were keeping watch, for in the next breath he opened his eyes and came to consciousness. Thereupon he lifted his hand and, reaching out, raised it slowly upward until his arm was fully outstretched and his fingers strained to touch the canopy. Yet almost in the same breath his fingers curled, his eyes half closed and his arm sank back to his side— Afterwards, Hüttenbrenner asserted that your Uncle, having made his peace with God, had raised his fist in defiance of "the powers of evil." Since, however, Hütten. had kneeled beside the bed in order to slip his arm under your uncle's head, he viewed him only in profile. Thus he could not see, as I could, your uncle's countenance which, far from defiant, was utterly grave and beseeching. Just what your

Uncle asked for, I have no idea, naturally; but I suspect that it was something for which there are no words, something—Fist indeed! his hand was cupped as though holding a small bird. In my opinion what he asked for, and in fact *received*, was permission to die. In any case he had breathed his last. Thus Hütten. closed your uncle's eyes and kissed them, and then kissed his forehead, mouth and hands. He also asked to have a lock of your uncle's hair. Although I obliged him, I must say that the squeaking sound of the shears cutting through that tough tress made me shudder.

Well, of one thing you may be certain: the following day found your Uncle Johann, Breuning and Schindler foregathered at Schwarzpanier House to search for the bank shares. According to your Uncle Johann, after they searched in vain for almost two hours, he threw up his hands and demanded that Breuning produce the shares! (As you well know, your Uncle Ludwig often said that there was someone, other than yourself, who knew where they were hidden.) Since, however, Breuning had no idea of their whereabouts, he was quick to take offense again. This provoked a nasty scene fraught with charges and countercharges, naturally. Just what your Uncle Johann thought Breuning had to gain by concealing their whereabouts, I cannot imagine. In any case once peace was restored, it occurred to Breuning that the unnamed person might be Holz. That, of course, did not sit well with Schindler who, needless to say, despises Holz and continues to regard him, even now after your uncle's death, as his archrival. Notwithstanding Schindler's objections, Holz was sent for. No sooner did the rival appear than he went to the credenza, released an unseen latch and voilà! a hidden compartment sprang into view. In it were found not only the seven bank shares, but also a love letter (whose tone, I may say, is ardent) and two miniature portraits—one of Countess Guicciardi and the other of an unknown woman whom Schindler takes to be Countess Erdödy. Had you any prior knowledge of such a love letter? In all likelihood it was addressed to one of the Countesses—the question is, of course, to *which of them*? Seeing that the salutation "My angel" tells us nothing and that the letter was never posted, nor for that matter was it dated—Well, you can just imagine what sort of grist this will bring to the gossips' mills!

Later that day an autopsy was performed by a certain Dr. Wagner. When your Uncle was lifted from the deathbed the bedsores, about which no one had ever heard him say a word, were so ghastly that Dr. Wawruch, who witnessed the dissection, covered his eyes in dismay. I needn't remind you how I feel about autopsies; ever since your Uncle took it into his head that I had poisoned your father— well, now it was his turn! Forgive me for saying that, it sounds so pitiless and vengeful. In truth when I saw for myself how horribly Dr. Wagner had disfigured your uncle's face (to explore the organs of hearing a portion of his skull and jawbone had to be removed) I, too, covered my eyes. Even if I were able to recall everything your Uncle Johann told me about Dr. Wagner's findings, it would take far too long to report here. Besides, you'll read the document yourself someday. Suffice it to say that your uncle's liver had shrunk to half its proper size, had turned a greenish blue color and was beset with knots the size of kidney beans!

The following day Breuning who, you will remember, took such umbrage at the idea of an artist sketching the dying composer, gave permission nonetheless to another artist not only to sketch the corpse but to fashion a death-mask—God in heaven! You cannot possibly imagine how sunken were your uncle's cheeks, nor how dreadfully the flesh sagged, hung down like dewlaps! Indeed the face was all but unrecognizable, yet Breuning decided that a death-mask—Enough! As for the sketch, it is simply ghastly; the eyes seem covered with cobwebs and the gaping mouth shows the teeth! In short, it is so gruesome that I swore never to look at it again. Still, there is one thing to be said in its favor: it depicts your Uncle with a full head of hair. Not that he was later shorn like Samson, but somehow or other, despite the constant presence of Sali and two attendants from the church, while your Uncle was lying in state, one mourner after the next helped himself to a lock of hair. Believe me, his hair looked like a cornfield after harvest; and the ill-effect was only somewhat mitigated by the wreath of white roses that adorned his head. With regard to the coffin, I suppose one might character-ize it as handsome or, better still, dignified; in any case it was pur-chased with leftover funds from London. Thus it fulfilled to a T the Philharmonic Society's stated purpose which, as your Uncle Johann reminded me, was to provide "comforts and necessities."

As for the funeral, I neglected to mention that when the coffin was carried downstairs there was such a crush in the courtyard the gates had to be locked. Those who were left outside burst into angry protest.—I will say this much for Breuning, at least he had the fore-sight to request some troops from the Alser barracks. (Is that not where you received your physical examination? It now seems so long ago.) In the courtyard were assembled a goodly number of priests as well as eight singers from the Italian opera company, including Cramolini! Once the priests had blessed the dead man, the Italians sang a chorus from *William Tell*. Considering your uncle's opinion of Rossini, I had to suppress a smile.—In addition to the Italians there were sixteen other singers, the best in Vienna, and four trom-bonists who played a piece your Uncle wrote in 1812 while visiting (to gloss the matter) your Uncle Johann at Linz. There were, more-over, eight Kapellmeister, including Kreutzer and Hummel, and I don't know how many torch-bearers. Among the latter were Grill-parzer, Schubert and Hüttenbrenner, the cloth merchant Wolf-mayer, Schuppanzigh, Linke, Weiss and Holz—Since Schindler served as a pall-bearer, a duty more notable than torch-bearer, doubtless he condescended to tolerate his rival.—Now try to imag-ine grouping all those people into some sort of orderly line. Well, when it was finally accomplished the Italians shouldered the coffin and the procession set out for the church.—How far would you say that Schwarzpanier House is from Trinity Church? 600 paces? 700? Whatever the distance, venture a guess as to how long it took us to arrive there. Half an hour? Forty-five minutes? It took no less than an hour and a half—so many spectators were there along the way. Why, even the schools were closed! Your Uncle Johann esti-mated the crowd at 20,000, the newspapers put the figure at 10,000.

At the church the crush was even worse than it had been in the courtyard. Again the troops were called upon to hold back the crowd; unfortunately they held *us* back, too! Not until we brought to their attention our black crepe bands and beautiful corsages did they believe that we were members of the family.—Once inside, it was all but impossible to move, let alone breathe; indeed three or four people fainted and had to be taken across to the hospital! I myself felt faint during the blessing; no doubt the closeness of the crowd, the censer and candles—Ah! I almost forgot to mention the candles. Never have I seen so many; there must have been a thousand, and all of them paid for by Wolfmayer. But candles aside, you may be sure that I heaved a sigh of relief when at last the Italians bore the coffin through the nave and out the door. Thank goodness they were spared the strain of having to bear it to Währing; a hearse, drawn by four horses, brought it there.

At Währing the coffin had to be carried into the parish church and blessed yet again, naturally! Then the procession moved on to the cemetery, yet only as far as the gates. There, to my surprise, the Italians set the coffin down. (Evidently it is forbidden to recite a funeral oration on consecrated ground.) In the next moment Anschutz stepped forward. Well, need I say more? Indeed all his mastery and emotion, nay, inspiration were put at the service of Grillparzer's words. For my money no actor in Vienna can touch him; there was not a dry eye in the crowd, as the saying goes.

Only then did I become aware of the *hush*; for the first time all day there was not a sound to be heard—not a church bell, not a birdcall. As we filed silently into the cemetery I realized that I was drying my eyes with the handkerchief that I had given your Uncle before he died. At the grave I found myself rehearsing a particular statement of Grillparzer's: "they called him malevolent." (Make no mistake, he was only speaking of those who didn't know your Uncle; for his part Grillparzer was altogether laudatory, praising the man as a great artist, a master, immortal, etc.) Since, however, I myself had called him that, malevolent, the week before he died, I felt remorseful.—And yet *he was malevolent*—Yes, of course he was all those other things as well—a great artist and a master, naturally! And more, much more; things that neither Grillparzer nor Goethe himself could ever put into words—But on the other hand—Dear me, clearly my feelings are mixed with regard to your Uncle.

When it was my turn to sprinkle the coffin with earth—I don't know what came over me, but all at once I began to cry—uncontrollably! I, who pride myself on self-control; not only did I cast the earth into the grave but also the handkerchief! Well, you may be sure that that did not escape the notice of Fat Stuff; she was consumed with curiosity.—What exactly did the gesture mean? Did the handkerchief have some personal significance? etc. I said only that by casting the tear-soaked hanky into the grave, I had hoped to put an end to tears—Indeed! Of what world could I have been thinking?

By the time we left the cemetery it was twilight.

Your loving mother

TITLES IN SERIES

For a complete list of titles, visit www.nyrb.com or write to:
Catalog Requests, NYRB, 435 Hudson Street, New York, NY 10014

J.R. ACKERLEY Hindoo Holiday*
J.R. ACKERLEY My Dog Tulip*
J.R. ACKERLEY My Father and Myself*
J.R. ACKERLEY We Think the World of You*
HENRY ADAMS The Jeffersonian Transformation
RENATA ADLER Pitch Dark*
RENATA ADLER Speedboat*
CÉLESTE ALBARET Monsieur Proust
DANTE ALIGHIERI The Inferno
DANTE ALIGHIERI The New Life
KINGSLEY AMIS The Alteration*
KINGSLEY AMIS Girl, 20*
KINGSLEY AMIS The Green Man*
KINGSLEY AMIS Lucky Jim*
KINGSLEY AMIS The Old Devils*
KINGSLEY AMIS One Fat Englishman*
WILLIAM ATTAWAY Blood on the Forge
W.H. AUDEN (EDITOR) The Living Thoughts of Kierkegaard
W.H. AUDEN W.H. Auden's Book of Light Verse
ERICH AUERBACH Dante: Poet of the Secular World
DOROTHY BAKER Cassandra at the Wedding*
DOROTHY BAKER Young Man with a Horn*
J.A. BAKER The Peregrine
S. JOSEPHINE BAKER Fighting for Life*
HONORÉ DE BALZAC The Human Comedy: Selected Stories*
HONORÉ DE BALZAC The Unknown Masterpiece *and* Gambara*
MAX BEERBOHM Seven Men
STEPHEN BENATAR Wish Her Safe at Home*
FRANS G. BENGTSSON The Long Ships*
ALEXANDER BERKMAN Prison Memoirs of an Anarchist
GEORGES BERNANOS Mouchette
ADOLFO BIOY CASARES Asleep in the Sun
ADOLFO BIOY CASARES The Invention of Morel
CAROLINE BLACKWOOD Corrigan*
CAROLINE BLACKWOOD Great Granny Webster*
NICOLAS BOUVIER The Way of the World
MALCOLM BRALY On the Yard*
MILLEN BRAND The Outward Room*
SIR THOMAS BROWNE Religio Medici and Urne-Buriall*
JOHN HORNE BURNS The Gallery
ROBERT BURTON The Anatomy of Melancholy
CAMARA LAYE The Radiance of the King
GIROLAMO CARDANO The Book of My Life
DON CARPENTER Hard Rain Falling*
J.L. CARR A Month in the Country*
BLAISE CENDRARS Moravagine
EILEEN CHANG Love in a Fallen City

* *Also available as an electronic book.*

ALAN GARNER Red Shift*

WILLIAM H. GASS On Being Blue: A Philosophical Inquiry*

THÉOPHILE GAUTIER My Fantoms

JEAN GENET Prisoner of Love

ÉLISABETH GILLE The Mirador: Dreamed Memories of Irène Némirovsky by Her Daughter*

JOHN GLASSCO Memoirs of Montparnasse*

P.V. GLOB The Bog People: Iron-Age Man Preserved

NIKOLAI GOGOL Dead Souls*

EDMOND AND JULES DE GONCOURT Pages from the Goncourt Journals

PAUL GOODMAN Growing Up Absurd: Problems of Youth in the Organized Society*

EDWARD GOREY (EDITOR) The Haunted Looking Glass

JEREMIAS GOTTHELF The Black Spider*

A.C. GRAHAM Poems of the Late T'ang

WILLIAM LINDSAY GRESHAM Nightmare Alley*

EMMETT GROGAN Ringolevio: A Life Played for Keeps

VASILY GROSSMAN An Armenian Sketchbook*

VASILY GROSSMAN Everything Flows*

VASILY GROSSMAN Life and Fate*

VASILY GROSSMAN The Road*

OAKLEY HALL Warlock

PATRICK HAMILTON The Slaves of Solitude

PATRICK HAMILTON Twenty Thousand Streets Under the Sky

PETER HANDKE Short Letter, Long Farewell

PETER HANDKE Slow Homecoming

ELIZABETH HARDWICK The New York Stories of Elizabeth Hardwick*

ELIZABETH HARDWICK Seduction and Betrayal*

ELIZABETH HARDWICK Sleepless Nights*

L.P. HARTLEY Eustace and Hilda: A Trilogy*

L.P. HARTLEY The Go-Between*

NATHANIEL HAWTHORNE Twenty Days with Julian & Little Bunny by Papa

ALFRED HAYES In Love*

ALFRED HAYES My Face for the World to See*

PAUL HAZARD The Crisis of the European Mind: 1680–1715*

GILBERT HIGHET Poets in a Landscape

RUSSELL HOBAN Turtle Diary*

JANET HOBHOUSE The Furies

HUGO VON HOFMANNSTHAL The Lord Chandos Letter*

JAMES HOGG The Private Memoirs and Confessions of a Justified Sinner

RICHARD HOLMES Shelley: The Pursuit*

ALISTAIR HORNE A Savage War of Peace: Algeria 1954–1962*

GEOFFREY HOUSEHOLD Rogue Male*

WILLIAM DEAN HOWELLS Indian Summer

BOHUMIL HRABAL Dancing Lessons for the Advanced in Age*

DOROTHY B. HUGHES The Expendable Man*

RICHARD HUGHES A High Wind in Jamaica*

RICHARD HUGHES In Hazard*

RICHARD HUGHES The Fox in the Attic (The Human Predicament, Vol. 1)*

RICHARD HUGHES The Wooden Shepherdess (The Human Predicament, Vol. 2)*

INTIZAR HUSAIN Basti*

MAUDE HUTCHINS Victorine

YASUSHI INOUE Tun-huang*

HENRY JAMES The Ivory Tower

STEFAN ZWEIG Confusion
STEFAN ZWEIG Journey Into the Past*
STEFAN ZWEIG The Post-Office Girl*